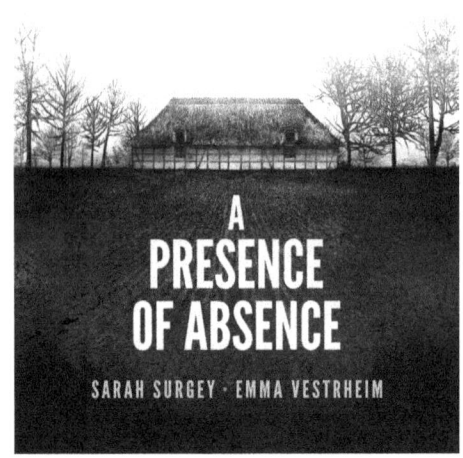

Cover by Mike Godwin

A Presence of Absence

By Sarah Surgey & Emma Vestrheim

After committing to my dream of moving from writer to author I knew that my family would be putting up with my constant writing at unsociable hours and living alongside highs and lows. But, we made it and in one piece, so thank you to my husband Mark, my daughters Holly, Phoebe, Tilly and Agatha & my parents Terry and Judy. Your support and willingness to help in anyway possible has made this a much easier journey.

- Sarah

To my husband Sean, for putting up with years of moaning by providing lots of love. Also to my parents, Greg & Lynette, for their enthusiasm and motivation.

- Emma

1981, near Faaborg, Denmark

The angel plucks a large handful of flowers, and they carry it with them up to God, where the flowers bloom more brightly than they ever did on earth.
- *The Angel, Hans Christian Andersen*

The farm was eerily quiet. The animals were sleeping and recuperating from dealing with the harsh weather which the day had brought. The landscape surrounding the farm painted a very imposing background, and this only added to the desolate position it was perched in. Farms in Denmark were sparse but necessary to the country's survival, or so it seemed. The isolated spot of this farm had only increased the distance between its inhabitants and the local town. Although they were known, they were not always accepted and this sadly sat well with them.

The barn door slamming open and shut in time with the wind was the only sign that something had been disturbed there. The more the door called for help, the more it became withered until eventually, it started to hang slightly off-centre.

The man inside the farmhouse had just been tending to a stockpot which held the evening's dinner of stew, made two days before. It would be devoured again tonight, he was sure, through pure hunger rather than enjoyment. Hearing the barn door call its last and loudest scream, he hesitantly put on his boots and decided to head over to the barn to quieten it. With the rain slamming down on him from all angles as the wind picked up speed and direction, he felt like he was being pushed back, away from the barn. He called out suddenly, questioning who was there as it became apparent that the lock was hanging off the barn. Relieved that he had on instinct picked up his rifle as he left the cottage, he pulled it up closer to himself as he slowly made his way to the door.

In a flash the door threw itself open, as though to expose its visitor to what was inside. The man froze in position. The figure before him was still. Surrounded by the haystacks and wooden pallets which sent out a musty smell, the barn was a holding place for surplus requirements.

Heavy breaths were the only sound in this space now, but under the surface, there seemed to be silent cries and a heartbeat which was racing, trying to catch up with itself.

The man stumbled forwards and stood in front of it. Shaking uncontrollably, the man used his hands to feel the figure, following the outline of the face until he had memorised every inch. Not moving, the figure was open to this touch. It didn't resist the kindness which was being shown, the gentle touch. The dangling figure let the man work through his fear and sadness for some time. Suddenly the man let out a shrieking cry which stirred some of the animals outside who had gathered to watch.

Cutting the figure down from where it was hanging, he pulled the body close to him and fell to the floor with it, making sure he protected it from the fall. Turning the body towards him, he once again slid his fingers down the face, this time closing the bright blue eyes that were looking at him, and tried to turn up the mouth so that it didn't hint at the fear it had known moments before its passing.

As the body lay lifeless in his arms he wiped at the tears which had stained the cheeks of the figure, then cut the rope from his neck.

Running his fingers along the old scars on the body's wrists, the man was angered at himself for not seeing this before. A previous attempt had obviously been made to erase the hurt, but he had found this too hard.

Sitting in the barn throughout the night was comforting in a way. As the darkness erased the scene of death in front of him, for a few hours the man could sit in his own denial. Now the barn door only gave out a sadness: the shouting had gone. The man had found what he was supposed to find and the barn held this secret with dignity.

A PRESENCE OF ABSENCE

1

London, United Kingdom

With her father sitting alongside her, Sanne could almost feel his uptight Britishness holding him rigid in his seat. He was probably going through the preceding schedule minute-by-minute in anticipation to be able to leave. Detective Simon Weller was facing forward and waiting for the Christening to begin. Even though he was approaching his mid-fifties Sanne had never seen her father as an old man. He had always been extremely fit, despite the heavy fatigue which came with being the head detective in central London. She had never noticed her father growing old until now. She had always lived in denial that her parents would grow old and eventually leave her.

Looking past her father, she found herself staring at her Danish mother, a complemented contrast to her father was the only way Sanne could describe her parents. Sanne's mother didn't look straight ahead towards the front of the church, like her father. She instead gazed at the baby, her pale face resembling the sculptures of the angels that lined the cathedral. A smile spread gently across her Mother's face, giving insight into what nurturing thoughts could be going on in her mind. Sanne suddenly had an urge to leave the pew where she was sitting and join her mother, having her mother's soft touch wrap around her and remind her that everything was going to be okay.

Sanne closed her eyes to stop the tears flowing and by the time she had opened them again her mother was gone. The faces of the angels had turned back to their stone-cold appearance and the cathedral darkened from the incoming rain. She cursed herself for being so silly.

Dealing with her mother's death was just so painful and each day she found herself living with a very real and impending presence of absence filling the void where her mother should be.

Simon knew that Sanne felt her breakdown had gone unnoticed, but he had known what she was thinking from the moment they sat down together. It had been three months since they sat in the front row saying goodbye to her mother and his wife, and now they had returned to the very same place to welcome a new life into the world. Sanne had tried to convince her father that this was a good reason to make their first appearance in public since the funeral, but Simon hadn't bought into her philosophical reasoning. He had agreed to come to this for himself. It had been so long since he had spoken to his wife and he was now looking for anywhere with a remote connection to her. He just needed to hear her voice again, and as much as he didn't consider himself a religious man, he felt this building gave him a chance.

Emotional pain is an invisible ailment which can be covered up by the subtle upward turn of the mouth and kept silent by positive sentences. But it is a tangible hurt that finds its way to every part of the body and mind, which rears itself with the sunrise and hangs on throughout the day, refusing to be sidetracked. Yet people expect someone who has it embedded in them to just shake it off and leave it lying there. They are the people who had never experienced the intense feeling of loss. It is often looked upon to be treated like a physical problem, solved with medicine, but Simon knew this was often purely a placebo to comfort the outsider looking in. By the time they had arrived at the first social gathering since the funeral, Simon second guessed why he had agreed to come.

He was dealing with not only the loss but also the fact that she had wanted to take her own life. She was more than his wife; she was his soul-mate, as cheesy as he knew that sounded. The thought of having found her had not escaped his mind, and he could help but see her body lying beside him, whenever his head touched the pillow. This had caused him to lose night after night of sleep, and he knew it was showing on his face. Everything had been destroyed and none of it made sense. And he was in the line of work to understand scenes like this. He had cursed himself over and over that he had been unable to solve the most important case of his life.

The priest approached the pulpit and began to recite words from the bible. Simon closed his eyes and cursed, louder than intended, judging from the cold glances that had been shot his way.

"Can you please not do this now? Mum would have…" Sanne whispered, cutting off her sentence when she realised this was the first time her mother had been spoken about in the past tense.

"Don't tell me what she would've wanted" Simon growled, feeling more sets of eyes casting themselves over towards the grieving family. Simon left the cathedral, causing the floorboards to creak and the attention to drift from the priest to himself. He left in a hurry, hearing Sanne and her husband Michael following close by. His and Sanne's relationship had always been one of protocol and order. When to speak with emotion, and when to speak with just words. The latter was the usual path taken and Simon had often wondered, even discussed with Vibeke, whether this came from his career in the police force or his own nurtured personality which fed off self-righteousness. The right track. The right actions. The right conclusions. They brought calm with them of the knowing. Now he didn't know anything anymore.

He had always been regarded as someone who hid emotion. Even when the most gruesome cases were thrust in front of him, he always remained pragmatic and reacted with a level head, especially within the first few hours of a case, and he was known for putting on a front as to not worry his team, even when they knew he hadn't eaten or slept for 24 hours or had time to go home and reconnect with his family.

Everyone saw him as a cold-faced detective who used poor jokes to hide his grief. But the lines were blurred between work and home and he sometimes treated his children like one of his officers and on most occasions led from the front, leaving his wife at the back, nurturing and guiding the children. His son Thomas seemed to have thrived on this type of upbringing and looked to Simon as his role model, even though he had chosen insurance as a career. He now was working his way through the ranks at a quick pace: he had the strengths and morals of a detective, Simon always thought. Sanne, however, took the alternate route and pushed her father to his limits growing up. She had gone down the route of homemaker after many years before going off the rails, and found a husband named Michael who had a 9-5 job pushing a pen, also in insurance in the city, so "he would be home for his children to tuck up in bed," Sanne had shouted a few times, when she felt it necessary to hurt her father.

Simon was good at pretending and this had stood him in good stead when the pretence relied upon his acting being fond of this pencil-pusher his daughter had chosen to not only spend her life with but also bring two children into the mix of this storybook life which Simon felt would one day bring a not so happy ending.

But Sanne, he realised, felt it her duty now her mother was gone to take the role of someone who gave reassurance, guidance and motivation to her father and to see him through these dark days so he could suddenly miraculously come out from the depths of despair. She had no doubt been reading her many American self-help books and listened with intent to the gurus who seemed to be flooding the market to find the answer: to bring her dad back. She couldn't bring her mother back. So she was starting from a point of failure in Simon's eyes and had nowhere to go. This game of pretence would go on until Sanne was comfortable enough within her own lies to tell herself that her father was fine and on the right track. He would help her along if it gave him some peace with his own thoughts of Vibeke.

Out in the hallway, Simon fought back the tears as he read the flyers pinned to the message board. Alcoholics Anonymous, drug addict support groups, cancer survivor support groups, all the groups were there. He looked over to the one for those dealing with grief but turned away again immediately. He had never felt so alone.

"Dad, Kim is my best friend. She wants us here. Please can we stop making a scene?" he heard Sanne say behind him. He held back tears and refused to face her.

"I know" he muttered, folding his arms.

"What are you going to do, Dad? Fly to Denmark and forget about us? Forget all your troubles and leave us here?" Sanne said, almost shouting this time. Simon sighed. After three months of living on the couch surrounded by bottles of various liquors, Simon had booked a one-way ticket to the hometown of his wife, Odense in Denmark. He and Sanne had been fighting about whether or not to sell the second house they owned in the central Danish city, and as Sanne was winning the argument with real estate agents about to be booked, Simon had quit his job and booked the flight in a move to outbid his daughter. This had come as a shock to Sanne and she had been holding it against him ever since. He knew she felt abandoned after her mother had decided to take her own life and now that her father was leaving, but he couldn't bring himself to address this and instead the two had been fighting almost daily. He wanted to wrap his arms around her and tell her he wasn't going away like her mother was, but something kept holding him back, perhaps his pride.

Or maybe he just didn't want to care about anyone anymore. But now he was leaving tomorrow and this had no doubt caused tension on what was supposed to be a pleasant gathering.

Simon had never in his role of being a father put his feelings of unease onto his two children, but since Vibeke had passed he felt himself becoming childlike again, rash in his decisions and standoffish in his emotions. And the saddest part was that he recognised this, but he didn't have the strength to change it.

Simon's job was extremely demanding, not only on the body, with the long hours you put your heart and soul into until the job is done, but emotionally, by seeing the human race at its very worse. Somehow he had always managed to compartmentalise these emotions, but with this personal nightmare he was in, he found his emotions floating all over as if at sea, bobbing up and down to the rhythm of grief. Years of hunting down London's toughest criminals and visiting monstrous crime scenes had made Simon emotionally numb, and so in his wife's passing he had been able to maintain his façade. He was waiting for it all to come crashing onto the shore.

"Simon, how about I give you a ride home? I've got some work to do anyway" Michael, Sanne's husband, added to ease the tension.

"What? You mean you aren't staying either?" Sanne quipped, "I thought you said you could finish off tomorrow"

"No, you said I could finish off tomorrow. Sanne"

"You mean you don't want to be here, Michael? You didn't want to come from the start," whispered Sanne as her father turned to face the two of them. Michael's face dropped and he took a step closer into Sanne, towering over her.

"Sanne, don't take this out on me. I have a big project on at the moment and I have to finish it off as soon as possible. Simon clearly isn't coping. It will be for the best. You've got the kids and your brother still here" Michael whispered. Simon pretended he hadn't heard it and turned for the door.

"Come on, Michael. Let's go" he said briefly, avoiding eye contact with his daughter.

"Am I going to see you before you leave?" Sanne cried, but Simon didn't hear her. Feeling that the two men she trusted most were letting her down, Sanne returned to the cathedral to watch the new life being blessed into this world. Death often makes way for life, another cliché she had been told by a rather nosey but well-meaning neighbour who had learned about the passing of her mother as Sanne was congratulating Kim on the birth of her baby.

Sanne had wanted to scream then as she did now. Michael had let her down in the past couple of months, too. He had become distant and more indulgent in his work. Kim had said to Sanne one day that this was how men cope with their wife's grief. They felt like a spare part and knew that this time, they couldn't fix it. Sanne understood this logic but didn't like the practice. Michael hadn't always been there for her, but she could always rely on his advice. Recently, though, he had become so distant from her that she felt her burden was nothing more than an annoyance to him. Sanne looked up to the angels once more and told them to tell her mother she missed her.

*

Michael couldn't concentrate on anything else. His phone had not stopped buzzing since they had been at the christening. He just needed to get Simon home and then he could take the call. He had seen the look of disappointment in Sanne's eyes when he volunteered to drive her father home, but these past months he had been on the edge of most emotions with all of them.

London was ridiculously congested today and to get Simon from one side and then back across to the other was a logistical nightmare. Turning to his passenger on his left, Michael could see that he was barely holding it together. It was the right choice for him to come home, Michael thought. But he knew Sanne would be angry. She so needed her dad to be 'better'. Michael knew that as soon as Simon got back into his house, he would head upstairs to the bedroom and fall into bed. Hide from everything, but the strange thing was that was the place his misery hailed from. Where Vibeke ended it all.

Michael was going to speak with Sanne tonight; they needed to shake Simon out of this. Michael had far too much going on to ferry Sanne's zombie-like father around. Checking on him after work, listening to Sanne's frustrations every night. He couldn't bear to watch this drama for much longer. There was a time when Simon would have picked up on Michael's problems, taken him to one side and tried to help, for Sanne's sake of course. Michael was half-glad that Simon wasn't of sound mind at the moment, the last thing he needed was Simon on his back.

"Do you need me to come in?" asked Michael as Simon pushed

open the Land Rover door.

"No I'm fine, I have to pack. Do you still have the spare key?" Simon said in a short tone.

"Sanne has it" Michael replied quickly.

"Good. Just check on the place every now and again. Make sure it doesn't burn down and so on"

"Will do. Shall I see you tomorrow? I can take you to the airport?" Michael said, but Simon shook his head and left the Land Rover, as though to avoid the question altogether. With that, Michael watched the once-great London detective shuffle to his front door with his shoulders hunched and his head down. What a sorry state, thought Michael as he sped off to take his call. Not waiting until he got home, Michael pulled over to the side of the road and picked up his phone. He had twelve missed calls. Not from the man himself but from his people. Michael had never actually spoken with the boss, and that suited him fine. The calls were intense and demanding and Michael knew he had to do something about this.

Holding his phone in his hand as if he could just magic everything away by throwing it out the window, Michael suddenly had a realisation. These people weren't going anywhere, and he had nowhere to hide from them or his demons.

2

Odense, Denmark

How are you liking Denmark?

If for nothing else, he had come to Denmark hoping to avoid that question.

Simon's day had begun well; the early morning flight out of Heathrow had gone without delay or drama, and he had avoided Sanne's last-minute calls, no doubt an attempt to sway him to stay home. He had arrived in Copenhagen shortly before nine and had immediately transferred to Central station to take the next train out to Odense. Simon landed in the city by midday and had spent much of the afternoon feeling nothing but reminders of Vibeke.

The city of Odense always appeared to be covered by a misty haze. Positioned in the central Danish island of Funen, Odense was too far from the beach to be considered a seaside, too large to be considered a town, and too modern to carry the traditional Danish heritage which attracted tourists. Odense looked like any other European city and often served as little more than a centralised stopover between Copenhagen in the east and Aarhus in the north.

Simon had found himself in the Hans Christian Andersen museum when he had been asked on his thoughts of Denmark. This questions made him realise just how much he was stalling from heading out towards the house he and Vibeke had spent so much time in. Odense had a unique quality that had given it some likeability. It was the birthplace of Hans Christian Andersen and the city was sure to make that known. The parklands, the central streets, and the heritage homes all in some ways been attributed to the famous Danish writer, and it was for that reason that tourism in Odense over the last decade had boomed. Simon had always admired Vibeke's passion for the Danish writer. While most of their Odense friends cared little for the city's obsession, Vibeke had all the books and had made an effort to educate her British family in the history of Hans Christian Andersen and all the wonderful things he had done for Odense. Simon had never been much of a reader and found the fairy tale's silly.

Avoiding the question from the bubbly teenager behind the counter, Simon left the museum abruptly and found himself hit by the true feeling of autumn. Though it was only October, the rainy days had become more common, and as the nights descended upon the city early, the residents fled the shops and retreated into their warm and cosy homes. While Simon was used to the depressing weather that came from living north in Europe, he always felt as though Denmark was especially cold, despite it being not much closer to the North Pole than England. Copenhagen had not yet caught up to autumn, and as Simon had boarded the train from Copenhagen H, he was glad to see that maybe he had arrived early enough to miss the Danish chill. He recalled a September he and Vibeke set aside to renovate the cottage, but after ten straight days of rain they had given up and headed to neighbouring Nyborg for a glimpse of the sun. He was hoping, judging by the Copenhagen weather, that the forecast for Odense wouldn't reflect his mood about being there. However, as the train travelled west, through the tunnel and onto the island, he thought that he had been wrong and watched as the landscape descended into a drizzle.

Returning to the central station, Simon check timetable, hoping the bus he needed to take w: Upon realizing that it would be another forty-fiv could get on, he turned to the park that sat acrc sighing at the thought he needed to endure Ode

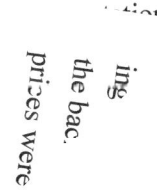

The autumn weather had turned the once green Kongens Have into a brown and dismal park, hardly a friendly greeting to the city centre of Odense. The mist had settled across the grass, and the rapidly approaching dark had made the park carry a sense of mysteriousness that would've made Simon feel uneasy if he was walking through any other park than one in Denmark.

Vibeke had loved Kongens Have, always mentioning the grandeur of the palace that sat in the centre. Simon had always thought that the Odense Palace never seemed rather royal. Dating back to the 15th century, Odense Palace, or Odensegård, as it was known back then, had served everything and everyone from the monastery to government operations. After the building became the property of the King, it was occupied by the Swedes in the mid-17th century. While Denmark managed to win the Odense Palace back and royalty remained, the governorate was terminated when the royals decided to head back to a warmer Copenhagen. And, as Vibeke liked to eagerly point out, Hans Christian Andersen had played in the palace gardens with Prince Frits, later King Frederik VII and his mother had worked in the palace. Simon always believed the old British palaces put this Danish one to shame.

The trees that hid the palace from public eye served more purpose than to shield the palace from judging eyes. They were placed well enough that Simon could rush through them and not have the rain drench them. Racing through the park, Simon noticed the theatre and across from it was a Chinese restaurant. Chinese restaurants were often quick, and Simon knew he could kill some time before the bus arrived.

There was no one in the restaurant except for a teenage girl looking bored at the counter. Simon entered through the door and sat in the corner. He picked up the menu and was relieved to find the similar to home, even if it did mean the quality would probably be lower.

From behind the counter the girl, who was clearly no older than fifteen, came over to him. She spoke something in broken Danish, and Simon sighed. He was hoping she'd speak English. Rather than try to talk, Simon pointed to the menu at what he wanted. The girl looked closely at the menu, confused, and said something in what sounded like Danish.

"No, no. Just the rice," Simon said, pointing to the faded image of what he was sure was rice. The girl was taken aback by the accent, but nodded and went to the kitchen. As Simon sat there taking in his surroundings he became aware of his thoughts relaying to him that his journey had been a bit of a blur. This had had nothing to do with the glass of Beaujolais he administered at Heathrow's bar before the flight. How can someone travel in a state almost of slumber? He had achieved just that, unnoticed. Apart from the woman next to him, who was stopped dead in her tracks of trying to start up a conversation with him before the flight had even taken off, Simon was sure that he had blended in with the ant trail of people mulling about getting from one destination to the other. The only moments of clarity that he could recall were going through security, which Simon noted had intensified immensely since he had last flown with Vibeke, but he probably looked more relaxed then than he did now and less like an uptight fanatic. The calming effect Vibeke had had on him was slowly showing itself to him.

After finishing up his rather stale bowl of rice, Simon made his way back through the park to the bus stop while lost in thought about how Sanne had pushed him into this journey. She was trying to jump into her mother's shoes much too early for his liking. Yes, Simon was in turmoil, he admitted that. But he deserved this turmoil; he should be punished for allowing Vibeke to fall so far. The splatters of the roadside puddle were the first sign that the bus had arrived, as it almost slapped him in the face to remind him of the journey he was about to embark on.

He hadn't been hungry really, he was just killing time. Before he would have to arrive at the cottage, alone.

As he sat on the late-night bus Simon surveyed his travel companions. Old habits die hard: this was embedded in him as a detective. Know the people around you; study them and watch them. Where did they come from? Where are they going? And what are they saying? You never know when this would have to be relayed. Vibeke always jolted him out of his obvious staring, but now he didn't give a shit. God, was that how he would go forward... not giving a shit?

The woman in front of him was sitting in fright, not from the other passengers per se, but from her own mind's eye. The way she held her handbag tightly to her body, the constant need to stare at people trying to suss them out but dropping eye contact in an instant if she felt they were looking at her. Poor lady probably wasn't even comfortable in her own home anymore: fear can do that to you and it seems to grow in stature the quicker the years roll on.

At the back but taking centre stage were three teenagers. The type whom the lady in front would cross the road to avoid. They weren't particularly harmful and Simon could not understand all of what they were saying but he could tell that their presence was making certain passengers feel uneasy. The teenagers were two boys and a girl, all probably around fifteen years of age, but the girl with her make-up on obviously wanted to portray someone older.

To Simon's right were two men of darker skin who he presumed were speaking in Arabic. Simon had learned to recognise this language since the area in which they lived in London over the last couple of years had had an influx from Arabic-speaking countries. He had no problem with this really, he was just aware of the tensions that were sometimes caused. Simon did, however, note that the two men seemed to be on edge themselves and when they came to a somewhat unsavoury part of town they quickly stood up and made a quick exit off the bus, which seemed to relax the shoulders of the lady passenger in front.

With the suburbia of Odense becoming more and more familiar, he couldn't help but feel anxious about the approaching cottage he had left behind. Simon turned to the seat beside him to pick up the old newspaper that had been left behind. He unfolded the scrunched-up paper and studied the cover. He cursed himself for not learning Danish earlier, but immediately picked up the word 'overfald'. When he and Vibeke were younger, Simon had become involved in a gruesome case that almost drove him out of the job. Vibeke had tried to convince him to relocate to Denmark where there were fewer crimes. She had taught him some of the keywords he'd need to know, and he had almost convinced himself it was a good idea before he dismissed it and went back to work. He didn't want to be seen as weak then just as he didn't want to be seen as weak now. He scrunched the paper back up and looked out of the bus window. The street was approaching and in unison, to this, he told himself that he could do this.

Walking along Svanevej, Simon kept his head down and away from prying neighbours. They had made some friends over the years – well, Vibeke had made friends with her neighbours and he always avoided the Danish conversation. The people around here were proud of their middle-class lives and Vibeke had admired that. Simon thought this to be part of the reason she had chosen a place out in the suburbs and not a contemporary mansion on the riverfront in town. But rather than choose something that needed nothing doing to it, they chose the one looking for some love and attention and had all the intentions to provide it with that.

Looking at it now, the building told a story of loneliness, hardship and finally defeat. Simon had wanted to move on before they even stepped up the path, but Vibeke had wanted to give it a chance. Hear its story, nurture it back from ill health. She saw this beneath the layers of decay and despair as a place for them to bring their young family to so they could absorb some happy energy into the four walls. Simon remembered that this could well have been the first disagreement in their relationship. But Vibeke had the strings to his heart and Simon knew that any disagreement would be pointless, as in the long run, his wife's happiness was what got him through his days.

The dim streetlights were just enough for Simon to be able to see as he took the first tentative steps up the path and found the wall to hold onto and grab when he stumbled after seeing Vibeke's little car parked neatly in front of the garage waiting for her so patiently to start it up and guide it around these familiar streets. Not to be.

The key went in the first time and Simon wondered why he had doubted it would.

The smell was what hit him first. The sweet smell of Vibeke that had been missing from his senses.

He needed to sit down and in a panic and with his heart racing Simon flung open the door to the living room and slumped in a chair. Empty, lost and broken, Simon froze in the chair for the night. Not daring to move, not wanting to remember, not wanting to see another reminder that she had gone. He closed his eyes and felt as though he was being reunited with her at last.

3

London, England

Michael wandered through the streets after declaring he needed to pop out to buy some milk for the next morning. He had found himself emptying out the remaining contents of what milk they did have left just to back up his story. Desperate times, he thought to himself.

He needed to make a phone call and didn't want Sanne hearing it. Sanne had never been interested in his business, at least not until he started given her a reason to follow him day after day. He wasn't blind; he could see his attitude was only adding tension to Sanne's life, which he had undoubtedly made harder.

Opening the gate to a small park nearby, Michael subdued the creaking hinges and closed it silently behind him. He sat on a nearby bench and observed the rapidly coming dark; summer was well and truly over. He unbuttoned the top of his shirt and puffed it out: London could still be so humid in the colder months. He wiped the sweat from his brow and took a long, deep sigh. Placing the bag of groceries at his feet, he pulled his phone from his pocket and stared at it. He dialed the number he had come to know only too well and waited for the response.

After what seemed like forever his call was finally answered. The abrupt receiver on the other end quickly passed him over to whom he should be talking to.

"I need more time" Michael blurted out "Please, you need to give me more time." The man on the other end had no sympathy for Michael. They dealt with people like him every day. They were hard and callous and dealt in money not emotions.

"Your time is running out." the voice said, a threat of danger in his tone.

"I've tried everything" Michael shouted, "I've ruined everything."

But the line went dead and Michael was left sitting there, frozen in his own fear with the phone still pressed against his ear. He felt tears forming but quickly wiped them away along with another round of sweat, and picked up his groceries. Sanne would be waiting for him now; he had taken longer than she would have anticipated. She was always searching, looking into his eyes for some deception. She didn't trust anybody anymore and Michael felt he only had Simon to blame.

He found it comforting to place the blame on those who couldn't fight back anymore.

4

Odense, Denmark

Getting off the bus from visiting her friend, Avilda decided that she would be okay if she hurried along at a fast pace. She had always heard that Denmark was the safest country in the world, but watching the current affairs programs that told stories of youth gangs, immigrants, and drug mafias, Avilda had succumbed to the headlines and had grown paranoid in her old age.

She was never out this late at night but her friend was ill and had insisted that she needed company tonight. With her friend being at the centre of most things in their church, Avilda knew that if she didn't oblige her unChristian attitude would be the talk of the church by the following week.

Avilda hadn't enjoyed her bus ride. The teenagers were disgraceful in their language and she was sure that the two foreign men had been keeping an eye on her handbag from the moment they had got on. She was relieved when they had exited the bus but had stayed on high alert because of the other man who was sitting near to her seemed to be scoping out the bus and its passengers.

The bus had only taken her so far and now all she needed to do was get one more bus to take her the short two stops home. She could probably walk the distance but the dark scared her and she would much rather be around people this time of night.

Odense was her hometown, she grew up here and knew every street and alleyway that there was snaking around the city. Quite often she would sit outside the local cafe and watch the tourists walk up and down, looking only for Hans Christian Andersen related places. Yes, that was all very well and good, the man had been a very successful writer, but there was so much more to this place than just him.

Realising she was approaching the bus stop whilst lost in thought, Avilda took the turning on her right and looking down at her watch thought to herself that she would only have to wait around five minutes before she would be safely on the final leg of her destination home.

Her husband used to say that the evenings in Odense brought to life a city which otherwise often fell into the shadow of Copenhagen. She couldn't remember when they had ventured in to enjoy themselves in their married life but smiled at his outlook on things which were dear to him.

The rain was starting to fall, not heavy but just enough to cause a fine mist which was only highlighted by the lamp posts along the back streets. Scolding herself for not bringing out an umbrella, Avilda started to look around inside her bag for something which she could put over her hair for cover. Pulling a neck scarf out she started to tie it over her head, still trying to hold on to her bag and bus pass she could feel herself starting to feel flustered. It didn't take much to shake her and when things started to go wrong she could feel herself fretting.

Quickening up her pace so she would not miss her bus she noted in her mind how dirty some of the streets were becoming. There were cigarette butts and discarded rubbish littering the curbs and she couldn't count how many times she had nearly trodden in dog muck.

"Nearly there," she told herself, "just one more corner."

As Avilda turned the last corner her feet fell immediately from under her, she screamed as she went down but it wasn't until much later on the next day that she realised her screams came out in silence as the shock strangled their noise.

The body was hanging there, swinging in the mist. There was no doubt what she was seeing. It had to be a woman, judging by the slender physique, which was limp and so out of place. She couldn't see the woman's face as it was covered in hair and what skin was visible, had turned blue from the hanging. Avilda's hand went to her mouth as her other hand went to the mobile phone she had given in and bought only a few weeks before.

"Hello, Yes I need an ambulance. Now!" she shrieked. "There's a woman. She's hanging, from a lamp post. She's dead".

5

Odense, Denmark

As the rain fell against the window, Simon tried to get some sleep. Lying in bed, he wiped the sweat from his brow and rolled over. While his children had tried to persuade him to stay in London, he had convinced himself that moving to Odense would be easier. He was starting to question that as everything in this home reminded him of Vibeke.

Simon was suddenly jolted from his thoughts by the sound of the telephone next to him. He wasn't quite sure why the portal to him from helpless beings was still ringing; he had hoped it wouldn't work in another country.

"You need to learn to use your phone, I was getting worried" Sanne did admittedly sound worried, but Simon didn't seem to recall when she had been put in charge of his life.

"Sanne, it's late" Simon responded, opening his eyes.

"Oh, I forgot the time difference," Sanne said rather sadly.

"What did you need?"

"I just wanted to make sure you made it there safe."

"Safe and sound."

"That's good" silence fell between the two, then Sanne reluctantly added, "I spoke to the agent earlier"

"I don't want to do this now, Sanne"

"We don't have much of a choice. Please just do this for me. Thomas said it's a money pit at this point. We can't afford to keep it"

"Where do you think I am?"

"I… I know, dad"

"It's not a money pit if it's in use"

"Dad, you aren't seriously considering staying there?"

"I don't know, Sanne. All I know now is I want one night's sleep." Simon hung up on his daughter. He regretted it almost immediately but knew any attempt to call her back wouldn't work.

Looking around the room, Simon closed his eyes and tried to block out the visions of Vibeke's corpse. Even in another country the vision of her lying there motionless couldn't escape him. He opened up his phone and looked at a photo the two of them had taken together on a holiday in Spain. Simon stared into the face of the young, blonde beauty. Vibeke came not far from the city of Odense in Denmark. They had met back in a very cold winter just outside Odense. Simon had been coerced by a colleague, Gavin, from Paddington Green Police Station to venture to this unknown land for a visit to the fjords in October. Simon had been reluctant, but after weeks of having local 'must see' attractions rammed down his throat and as he was running out of excuses, the naive and young Simon agreed to accompany his overly enthused colleague.

Upon arriving in Odense, they were quick to discover that they were thinking of the wrong Scandinavian country when it came to fjords. The ten days they had set aside to explore now seemed empty, and while Simon had originally been annoyed, the two young men had instead found humour in their misfortune and took it upon themselves to enjoy whatever it was that Denmark offered. With that, they found that the best fun came from alcohol. Images of pretty blonde girls falling over themselves to welcome male tourists from afar and a somewhat sparse landscape were quickly put to rest as the rather large woman who greeted them at their hotel was no Danish beauty and Odense was just as bustling with close to 190,000 inhabitants. However, the beautiful Danish façades and architecture certainly distanced itself from Paddington Green's local streets.

It wasn't until five days into their trip that they made the fateful decision to leave the dilapidated hotel and head off to a restaurant they had been recommended by a rather drunk local the previous night. The restaurant was unassuming and in all honesty been sitting on any in any European country, but it was busy and they were starving, so they directed themselves in and were prepared to spend an evening of pretence, making small talk and enjoying quiet moments to people-watch while they ignored the awkward silence which had fallen upon them too many times on this trip.

As they entered the restaurant, which in Simon's mind was merely a pub with some small, wooden tables pinned into the corner as a place of pretense so the diners were not guilty of frequenting a pub most nights but a restaurant, he was struck by the noise of a confusing language. Vikings were the forefathers of this nation and Simon thought that the fashion had continued well into the 80s, with plenty of towering men proudly sporting beards and leather ensembles.

Slightly overwhelmed by the testosterone oozing from every corner of this eatery, Simon and his travelling partner decided to try and become invisible somewhere in the corner, down a few beers, eat quickly and get back on the road back to Hotel Hygge, as they sarcastically referred to it.

Trying their hardest to keep their English words to a minimum so as not to stir the locals, they sat in a welcome silence pretending to be enjoying watching the local spectacular perform their usual drunken nights out in front of them. It was this moment when a soft voice entered his personal space, and as Simon looked up he was greeted by a young lady who he realised was the Danish poster girl whom he had been anxious to see. Little did he know that this lady whom fate had brought to cross his path that evening would be the biggest part of his life, would follow him eventually back to London and would do him the honour of gifting him two children. After a few awkward moments of realising that he was intensely listening to her asking them what they would like to drink, in Danish, just because it sounded so pleasurable, the embarrassed Simon quickly explained in Danish that they were English.

Vibeke had a strange feeling inside of optimism. But what a funny feeling to have after only meeting a stranger for the first time. The thought of being able to see this man again was definitely stirring in her head. Grabbing the opportunity with both hands as she subconsciously rubbed her cheek where the night before she had received a blow from her father for failing to heat his dinner up adequately as her mother looked on out of the corner of her eye, not even having the guts to watch properly.

As the English guys were getting ready to leave, Vibeke took the chance so as not to let any of her father's friends see and scrambled a message on their receipt about meeting up on Pogestræde the next day. It was only thirty minutes by bus for her, but that was far enough for her parents never to venture to. This was crazy and she felt her odds were 50/50 about whether he would show, but fear did strange things to people's impulses and she wanted to escape this nightmare routine which she had lived in for so long.

She knew she was supposed to be somewhere else the next day which was very important, but she weighed up her options and decided that a letter would suffice. Maybe tomorrow would be the first day of the rest of their lives for her and her friend. She looked up as she thought this as if to get some recognition from God.

Outside, Simon smiled to himself: he was not expecting this beautiful waitress to show the slightest bit of interest in him. He was blown over when he got outside and realised that she had written a message for him on his receipt: he caught a glimpse of it as he pushed it into his wallet where he liked to file all his receipts. At first, Simon had to reassure himself from his memory that she had in fact insisted on putting the receipt into his hand so he could rule out the possibility that the message had been meant for Gavin.

Noting that his friendship with Gavin was becoming more strained by the hour on this trip, Simon, who always aired on the side of caution and had never in his life reacted on impulse, decided that he would make this meeting point tomorrow. He suggested to Gavin it would be best if he went off elsewhere as time was running out for their trip and Simon was sure he hadn't seen all that was on his checklist.

Simon made the excuse of wanting to take a long walk the next day for some fresh air and headed off to his appointment. Little did he know that this appointment would be the most important date of his adult life so far, as he would connect with a girl who would become his second half, his best friend, the love of his life, his wife... till death do them part.

Forcing himself back to sleep as he remembered that the next day was to bring him a new challenge, something that he had initiated on a pure whim, Simon mind once again allowed the nightmares to creep in.

The forest fell silent as she walked along the path which was opening up for her. Her blonde hair was highlighted further by the early evening sun which was winding its way down through the trees.

As she moved forwards Simon felt like she had a purpose. He didn't know why he was sensing that but he continued to enjoy watching her from up above. She carried on with her journey and he noticed how the animals around her stood back and watched her presence in awe.

Vibeke soon stopped when she came to a clearing and Simon again had a sense of her intentions. She knelt down when she came to a pile of sticks which seemed to have fallen into a heap at the end of the pathway. Confused, Simon squinted as if that would give his eyes more insight into what she was about to do.

As he focused solely on her face, Simon was taken aback by her expression. He had never seen her like that before. Her face was contorted and lines of anger were across her forehead as she scowled whilst looking down at the ground.

With slow purposeful movements, Vibeke now started to unpick the pile of sticks one by one and place them next to her. As the sticks moved away from where they had been lying they unearthed what looked like another pile gathered up together by the forest inhabitants.

Leaning forwards Vibeke started to frantically dust away at the pile which was under the sticks. Her motions were definite and Simon could tell she was fixated on what she was doing. Suddenly she stopped and Simon heard her speak for the first time and as she uttered words.

The shock of hearing her voice woke him with a start.

Trying to force himself back to sleep once more so he could hear her voice again Simon became frustrated that he could not achieve that but he took comfort from being able to hold on to what he had heard, for most of the day, until her voice faded away.

"There you are" she had said. That he was sure of.

6

Odense, Denmark

The chief of the Funen Police had just been heading home to his wife when the call came in. It was rare that calls came through in the night-time, and while Waage Bøttger didn't mind working late, it was seldom that he spent his evenings doing more than paperwork and briefing various officers on work ethics. The calls he usually received at night came from young officers working the night shift, unsure how to respond to an illegally parked car or a drunk reveller shouting obscenities out in the centre of the Odense shopping district. Waage had grown into the knowledge that not a lot happened in Funen, and nor should it. Denmark was a safe and rich country, he proudly believed.

The officer on the phone stated plainly that the town's busybody, Avilda, had discovered a dead body on Munkemøllestræde. She had shrieked into the phone that Waage and Waage only needed to get down there. Waage always liked his celebrity-like status in the town but felt as though it hindered more than helped when it came to circumstances like this.

Waage hung up and immediately dispatched more officers to the scene. He then dialed through to Romain, one of the newer Politi cadets to join the Funen Police and easily the stand-out of the whole crime department. If anyone could solve a case quickly, it would be Romain. Romain came from an Afghan family, and his parents had arrived in Denmark when he was a small boy. While he grew up in a lower socio-economic background and this often led young immigrants to gangs and violence, Romain maintained a positive attitude that he wanted to show his community that it was possible to make something of themselves in a country that was so resilient to change. Waage admired his work ethic and Romain was a well-respected figure in Odense. But more than that, he was an exceptionally talented detective and a discovered woman's body was something Romain could solve.

Arriving at the scene, Waage instantly spotted Romain and motioned him over. The scene had already been cordoned off and the police were studying the body, which was hanging from one of the various lamp posts that lit an otherwise dark street. Romain recounted what he had gathered: Avilda had been travelling between one bus stop to the next when she had come across this young girl hanging from the lamppost. After managing to phone for help, she had collapsed from shcok. It was lucky that a young couple had come across both the women. Avilda was still in shock so had been taken off to the hospital to be checked over and a female officer had eventually accompanied her home. Waage listened as he tried to figure out what to do with the case, concluding it could be something to do with the rising gang violence he had heard about just a month ago while in Copenhagen attending a conference, however, for this to be a young female was slightly left field.

"Thank you, Romain. Call Bengt up and make sure no one touches the body." Waage said, pulling out his mobile phone to make some notes to follow up with Bengt. Waage was the most senior rank at the scene, and he felt confident that he had allocated and notified the correct people, and now the case will be hushed quickly. "Have we identified the victim?" he added, not paying attention to the body hanging from the nearest lamp post.

"Elsbet Sørensen. It's hard to identify her as her face has turned from the hanging, but Avilda recognised the girl from church. She asked when you were coming down. She seemed to want to speak to you"

"Sørensen?" Waage asked, ignoring Romain's comment about Avilda. He had been used to listening to Avilda's complaints to the point where he had grown to not take them seriously. He knew he'd get nothing of use out the woman anyway; she'd use the opportunity to remind him about the growing threat of immigration and various types of drugs.

"Yes, the daughter of Martin and Emilia. Twenty-three years old, bright, a teacher at the boarding school just out of town" Romain said, glancing up at the figure hanging above them.

"I know who she is. Any reason to believe it was because of her name? Was she mugged?"

"Doesn't seem like it. All of the usual belongings are still on the body."

"Suicide, then?"

"Can't rule it out. Hangings are generally suicide related, but she's so high up. She couldn't reach that post easily. Didn't find any chairs or stools nearby. You'd need to speak to the parents."

"Have they been notified?"

"In the process of doing that now, but I suggest we take down the body in case they show up. They were dining at a friend's house nearby" Romain said, sarcastically stressing the word 'dining' and turning back to the scene as the officers took photos and gathered evidence.

"Don't move the body until Bengt arrives" Waage repeated sternly.

"Well here's the interesting part," Romain added, quietening his voice as if to keep it a secret from curious outsiders. Waage leaned in and listened to his detective explain that Elsbet Sørensen had been found with hay stuffed in her mouth. "Yes, the kind you'd find on a farm," Romain added. Waage told Romain to make sure there were enough photographs and to ensure that it stayed within those directly investigating the case. Romain was a talented officer, and while Waage would normally only take forensic information from Bengt, he trusted the young officer's opinion.

"Okay, finish up here and we'll meet first thing in the morning to discuss it all. I assume you'll have a full report on my desk tomorrow morning?" Waage said as he put his phone back into his pocket and reached for his car keys, somewhat eager to leave as the news vans were starting to park and the reporters were setting up their cameras.

"I can write up a report, but I'm on leave from tomorrow, remember? I have to go to a family wedding in Pakistan," Romain said, writing down some notes of his own. Waage sighed and remembered that Romain had built up some leave and he was cashing it all in during the supposed quiet period in Odense. His next-best in line, Ejnar, was on sick leave with no end in sight. Making a mental list, Waage stopped at the next name and felt a knot start to form in his stomach at the sheer incompetence that this officer would surely bring. But he was running out of choices and he needed this cleared up quickly.

Standing back and surveying the scene in front of him, Waage hoped this would go away quickly.

7

Odense, Denmark

Jonas Nørgaard was a man who was immensely proud of his heritage. 'Nørgaard' meant 'North Farm' and it was a name he did not take lightly. Jonas was made of strong stuff – both physically and mentally – and had stayed loyal to his Danish family heritage which for many generations had produced Nørgaard men who worked the land, harvested the crops that fed a nation and produced some of the best-prized animals in the area.

Jonas held the burden of not staying on his parents' farm once he was taken one day by the notion of protecting the local community. Jonas had by chance rescued a child from drowning in a local lake. He was immediately a local hero in this close-knit farming community and it even made the local papers. This eighteen-year-old boy had overnight become a grown man, and the attention and admiration stirred something in him which he hungered for even more. Farming was a way of life and would always be in his blood, but the determination to stay a hero was overwhelming and he felt like the only way to achieve this was to join the police force.

Jonas gained his degree and when he turned twenty-one set off on a path he felt had been given to him. Of course, it broke his parents' hearts, and throughout the rest of his life, he knew he would feel guilt whenever he visited. He knew one day the farm would be handed back to him if his parents managed to keep it afloat, and he spent many weekends there protecting his interest with physical work and financial advice.

Sometimes he felt this wasn't enough in his father's eyes. Jonas had wanted nothing more than to work on the farm and promised his father that once he had a family they would move back to the country and settle down on the property.

Jonas met and married his city-dwelling wife, Birgitte. She hadn't lived up to what his parents considered to be a good farming wife, and while Jonas had tried to teach her, the lack of interest had been mutual and she eventually refused to go out there. She had her own life in the city with the council Health and Safety Department. Not inspiring, not productive and not a title that Jonas' parents could quite understand; nevertheless, it paid the bills and kept a discreet distance between themselves which in turn suppressed the uneasy feeling of a mismatch, though this gave Jonas the time he needed when he wasn't working to 'do his own thing'.

That's how their marriage played out. It was a marriage of lust and then convenience. For Birgitte, as a young girl she had always dreamed of marrying a detective, and when she met the young student she admired his drive to serve the community. They married after three months of knowing each other, and over the years never spoke of children. Time went on and Jonas always expected it to be brought up; they watched as their friends raised children and Birgitte always insisted that careers were more important. She always hoped her husband's profession would outweigh any company that children could bring.

Jonas Nørgaard was now fifty-six years old and spent his days sitting in a police car counting down the minutes to retirement. He had never become the man either his wife or his parents had wanted, and now as his bulging stomach sat out in front of him and the wrinkles covered the majority of his face, he realised that he had never met anyone's standards. He had never worked up to the ranks of Police Commissioner, settling at the position of a traffic cop after the biggest mistake of his career.

When Jonas was in his early thirties, the rumours had started that he would be taking an over-the-top job any time now. He was assigned to a Serbian drug trade and many people, including Birgitte, told him that this was his one chance. He worked day and night trying to find enough evidence to arrest the kingpin, but nothing came and he could hear people starting to say that he wasn't up to it. Jonas ended up breaking into one of the dealers' apartments, and when he presented this evidence was punished instead of praised for his conduct and immediately transferred to the Motor Vehicle Department. It crushed his self-esteem and he never felt it come back. Birgitte gave up encouraging him and his life settled into a daily routine of eating alone and handing out tickets to people who sped through red lights.

Over the years he watched as young officers graduated from university and worked their way up and past his status. Watching this day after day always left a bitter taste in Jonas' mouth. Not a day's hard work in their lives and they would continue to float through the system working their way up. With their ideologies and technological knowledge, the younger generation who were flooding the police stations were policing differently, and Jonas felt an unease with this. In a way, he liked to work alone. Methodical and precise, taking his time not only to look for the obvious, but also to search for the not so obvious what was missing rather than what was there. He liked to get out into the community and feel what they were feeling.

Waking up early on a crisp autumn morning, Jonas put on his perfectly pressed uniform and took pride in his country as he looked out of the window as the sun was starting to rise over the small land he owned. He ignored a pain from his neck which had stiffened throughout the night after falling asleep in front of the television. He had finished a bottle of whisky and could feel the bitter aftertaste in his mouth, though it had become a regular affair.

The crime figures were at a new level in Denmark and it was this which kept him going day after day. He had awoken this morning to the newsreader stating that a murder had occurred in downtown Odense. Jonas couldn't remember the last time someone had been murdered in Odense, and he heard Birgitte mutter something about how Jonas should insist he be transferred to the criminal department to help out. Jonas didn't respond, but he thought to himself that the fact he was in front of the television and not called into the station meant they weren't interested. This was the second mugging and the first murder in such a short period of time and he couldn't help but assume who was causing all these crimes.

The only crimes he really had to be aware of in Odense were usually drunk locals who had grudges to bear, car rage around the tractors which still commandeered the back lanes, and rowdy teenagers who thought it was their rite of passage to intimidate younger children in the park. Nothing too major compared to other areas. Some might say Jonas was half the rank to the big city police and if he was ever to move from this area to police elsewhere he would be lowered, as his police years probably outnumbered his police experience.

Jonas thought differently. He was important, and the naïve attitude which the locals around him had would one day be their downfall, the crime was like cancer in the veins, moving slowly into position and hitting with vengeance when time could no longer hold back.

Foreigners were coming in and trying to change the dynamics, but Jonas would stand strong and respect the old ways. He had been sent on many awareness courses of late which were nothing more than a tick for the box so the do-gooders could satisfy their hippy ways and the police force could be shown that they were accepting and tolerant of a blended nation.

The less Denmark blended, the better. But that was an opinion

Jonas knew he had to keep to himself. There were friends and neighbours who agreed with him, he was sure, but they were all playing a game of make-believe. The pretence was a show which was performed more often than not. Pretence in the outside world of progression and intolerance. But the backstage dramas were more true to life.

Jonas put on his shoes and picked up his car keys. While the hunt for a murderer was on Jonas would protect the streets from a less scary criminal: red light dodgers and illegal parkers. What had his life become?

8

Odense, Denmark

The day had become with a numbing migraine Simon only had the wine to thank for. He had been visited by Vibeke in his dreams, and he had cursed himself for trying to think Denmark could rid him of those nightmares. Vibeke wasn't going to leave him, perhaps ever.

Simon had fallen asleep on the old patchwork sofa Vibeke had bought from her weekly trip to the flea markets. The sofa looked like it had seen better days, and that was especially shown in the comfort. Simon rolled over to reach for his phone and felt one of the remaining springs digging into his back. He knew he should've gone to the bedroom, which was only several feet away, but he was convinced Vibeke would find him there. He had been right, in a sense, but wrong about the location.

Turning on his phone, he noticed several text messages from Sanne about various topics. He deleted them, knowing he'd probably get scolded for doing so. Sanne had become a mother in the last few years, and as her children were now getting older Simon couldn't help but feel she was making him her next project – her next child. A toddler in desperate need of love and affection, and incapable of moving around freely.

Ignoring her pleas for attention, he moved over to a voice message from Waage Bøttger, the police inspector of Denmark's Funen Police Force and the man who had hired Simon. Simon hadn't told anyone in London this, especially Sanne. When Vibeke passed away he had quit his job with the Paddington Police, citing reasons that he'd lost his way if he can't even solve his wife's death. It had come as a shock to the community and to his family, but Simon hadn't cared. In between days of drinking and feeling sorry for himself, Simon had been reading the job boards in Odense, not knowing why or how that would do him any good. Nothing of use had come up, and after a particularly harsh argument with Sanne he had sent off his resume to the Funen Police, citing that he neither knew the language or believed he could be of any use. They must've been desperate because he was hired the following week.

Although Simon's orientation didn't start until midday, Waage told him to be in by nine. Waage hadn't said much on the phone, but Simon had been sure he could hear real concern in his voice. Simon rubbed his eyes and saw that it was already ten past eight, so begrudgingly he forced himself out of the sofa, which was trying to keep him there, and he put on some dirty clothes and left, leaving the front door unlocked. He told himself it was because he knew Denmark was a safe country, but perhaps part of him didn't want Vibeke's belongings there when he returned.

9

Odense, Denmark

After a grilling by one of the town's socialites, Jonas was fuming as he burst into the police station. The nerve of the woman, citing that she was disabled so that enabled her to park where she wanted to – no, needed to! She was no more disabled than she was discreet. The likes of women like her were, unfortunately, the heart of this town: they carried the blood to keep it regenerated and reproducing, they were the blackened veins in which it streamed, but in Jonas' mind they were what was wrong with this town.

Jonas was well aware of his volume and regretted shutting the station door that loudly: it only showed weakness that one of the towns trolls had got to him again, so he quickly tried to slow down his pace and make a more concerted effort to stop and smile at the rather lovely young receptionist that most certainly must be an outsider due to her fresh face and lack of any obvious inbreeding. God, he was becoming cynical.

Just as he was about to lead his way through the coded doors to go up to his desk and very laborious task of filling out a report on Mr Stengraas, who had wasted more of his time about some shrub stealing he felt he had fallen victim to for the third time in only two months, Jonas was stopped in his tracks by the receptionist whose name badge Jonas had now noted and would know her from now on as Trine.

Trine spoke with a Jutlandic dialect which confirmed Jonas' suspicions and sealed in his mind that he still had detecting skills when assessing people.

"Chefpolitiinspektor Bøttger has requested that you go and see him when you get back."

How had this receptionist realised he was who CPI Bøttger had meant? How had he been described? Jonas could only imagine. Waage Bøttger and Jonas had been fellow students at the police training headquarters in Copenhagen, albeit eight months apart. Waage was eight months ahead, so just when an eager, twenty-one-year-old Jonas had received his degree, Waage, who had already claimed quite a reputation as a man to watch who would undoubtedly rise through the ranks pretty quickly due to his family of police officers before him, was about to embark on his journey out in the big wide world with a job offer from Copenhagen. The eight months' difference in their training at that time had just felt frustrating, but Jonas naively believed they would always catch up – little did he know that that difference would put them worlds apart when they eventually stepped outside of training.

Jonas had never caught up and Waage's seniority had been lorded over him for many years now. At first, it started out as an uncomfortable gap between loose friends, but as the gap started to put further difference between who it meant they would socialise with, how much money they would make and how much notoriety they would gain, Jonas had become increasingly bitter about the whole eight months. Eventually, the awkwardness would settle down as Waage seemed to come to the conclusion one day that he would have to stamp his authority on Jonas and make it clear that he ran the department for this district and his second in command Ejnar Olsen was in fact, his right-hand man. After Jonas was transferred to a lesser department, Waage was finally able to assert the dominance and put Jonas in his place. The two had little to do with each other ever since, besides feigned friendly dinners with the wives.

Jonas could have swallowed this eventually, but what made this pill hard to swallow was the passing glimpse of pity Jonas caught in Waage's eyes; it was as if he actually felt sorry for his colleague below him and had a sense of duty to pull him long whilst coming to the hard decision that this battle would be in vain.

The town had not given them many pickings as young men who were eager to find a mate and settle down, so when Waage as a twenty-two-year-old police cadet took the one young girl who every man in the town had their eyes on, Lotte Andersen, it was a show of things to come.

In the time that Waage had finished his first nine months' training and come home to continue his next eighteen months before going back for his exams, he had managed to approach Lotte, date her and seal their love with an engagement ring. Those damn eight months.

Waage and Lotte were a devoted couple even to this day, and Lotte had remained loyal, kind and open to the life as a policeman's wife. She had often taken Birgitte to one side and tried on many occasions to engage in conversation about their roles and invite them over for dinner, but Birgitte found this all very sad that a woman would wage her self worth on her husband's job and frequently Jonas went alone. Jonas had often lusted after Lotte from afar growing up and when she blossomed into a beautiful woman Jonas felt she was quickly moving out of his league. Their parents had been neighbours in the country all Jonas' life, and he had grown up playing with Lotte in the wheat fields and as kids, they had been inseparable. As they entered secondary school, the teenage years and social status that came from that distanced the two; Lotte became a beautiful young woman and Jonas was the dorky farm boy who preferred to spend his time outdoors than at social dances. Entering university, Jonas and Lotte remained friends and it was through him that she met Waage. She showed Waage affection she had never shown Jonas, and before long the two were married and Jonas remained the third wheel, even in marriage with Birgitte.

The Odense Police Station was a modest building; to someone unfamiliar with the exterior they would think it just another in a series of apartments. In a sense, the exterior matched that of the need of the police in such a small city; with crimes seldom happening the police force didn't need to be large. The cosy quarters meant that everyone knew everyone, and there was always bickering about how neighbouring Nyborg got all the renovations and upgrades. Sometimes the Odense Police wanted to feel powerful, too. Despite this slight bitterness towards the neighbours, the Odense Police were highly respected around the town and had become a public image of a successful city, rather than a force to drive away criminals.

Romain had spent the night writing his report in as much detail as he could so the officer taking over had all the facts. He was looking forward to leaving the misty Danish autumn for the warmer weather of Pakistan, and while it had been suggested that he might be asked to stay, he had made it clear to everyone that the wedding of his sister was not one to be missed. He said that if the case was still going after the wedding then he would return; after all, he loved this city and all it had done for his family. This was the least he could do for Odense.

Excited by the prospect, Romain almost didn't see his relief turn up behind him.

"What exactly happened last night?" the voice behind Romain questioned. He turned around to see Jonas at the reception desk. Romain and Jonas had always got along, but Romain had never respected Jonas as much. He admired Jonas' stories of Danish farm life but always suspected that he had never liked the fact that a young Arab had become a more successful detective than he ever could, though this was something Romain never wanted to say out loud.

"Elsbet Sørensen was mugged and killed last night. Do you know who's on the case?" Romain said, watching as Jonas struggled to remove his coat.

"Good question. Waage's just called me up so maybe it's me. You and I working together at last!" Jonas joked, forcing a laugh that made his stomach shake. Romain laughed awkwardly and Jonas realised perhaps he wasn't as admired as he should be.

"I am on leave as of five minutes ago, so I'm handing it over. Must say I feel sorry for whoever is put onto this case, the Sørensen's being who they are" Romain said. Before Jonas had a chance to process the information, the young detective had dismissed himself from the conversation and left the station to go and enjoy his leave. What did Romain mean by that? Jonas felt his skin crawl as he realised this visit to Waage's office may not be what he had been hoping for.

As Jonas approached CPI Waage Bøttger's door, he felt his stomach start to churn. He was rarely called up to the top floor of the building anymore and he had allowed a sense of worry to creep in. Was he now surplus to requirements? Would he be sent on another hippy 'how to work with immigrants' course or maybe Avilda had put in another complaint against him.

For an older building, the top floor looked recently renovated and fairly polished; the brass name sign for Bøttger indicated to Jonas that he was now in a place of power. Much better than the cubicles offered to just the average police officer, Jonas thought bitterly to himself.

As he was about to knock on the door, Jonas noticed how he was second-guessing how many knocks he should do. One was quite weak but also showed you didn't need to announce yourself to the full degree and almost had an open door relationship; two knocks was more respectful; but three showed an air of confidence that you could knock on that damn door as many times as you liked because you weren't intimidated. Before he had a chance to come to a conclusion, Waage came out of the adjacent door behind him and looked with mild amusement at Jonas standing there looking like he was contemplating whether to even go in or not. Idiot, Jonas labelled himself.

"Come on in, Jonas. You'll get thread veins just standing there." Waage laughed.

He followed Waage into the office somewhat embarrassed and wondered how long Waage had been watching him stand there. Waage was known to watch his employees, and it wasn't uncommon to be in the middle of a rather long coffee break and look up to see Waage hovering over by the home-made biscuits. Jonas had always disliked this feature about his boss, as though Jonas himself and his work couldn't be trusted.

As Jonas looked over to Waage's oak desk, he noticed a man sitting there. The man was in rather dirty clothes and he could smell the alcohol from where he was standing. Jonas tried to recall his previous week on duty and if he had upset any drunks. He was known for his rather truthful comments but never thought they would come back to haunt him.

"Jonas, take a seat here," Waage said, pointing to the empty seat. Jonas was taken aback by Waage's English and stood there trying to translate the words.

"You do understand English, don't you?" Waage said, in a mixture of a condescending and sarcastic tone. Jonas nodded and obediently sat down. He glanced over at the stranger, unable to recognise him. Waage sat down and took a sip from his coffee and pulled a pastry out of his bag. Lovingly baked by Lotte, no doubt. Jonas thought about the canteen food that would greet him today, like every other day, as his wife Birgitte hadn't even begun the ritual of setting her husband up for the day with a good home-made lunch.

"Sorry, I had a very early breakfast this morning," explained Waage, excusing his need to eat and talk at the same time. "I would offer you something, but Lotte was rather slack this week and only made a few goodies" he added half-heartedly, but his smile shrank when he saw no one laughed in return. Waage was an attractive man by Danish standards. His face was well defined and his grey hair only added to his charm. Standing higher than Jonas at almost two metres, he looked like an actor constantly blessed with good luck and positive energy. He hadn't aged much since the two had been at school together, yet middle age had hit Jonas hard and he had developed his beer gut and was beginning to gain a hunch.

"A body's been found" Waage announced after taking a bite from his pastry.

"A person?" Jonas asked, dumbfounded.

"Yes. A human body" Waage rolled his eyes. "It was discovered on Munkemøllestræde, near the childhood home of Hans Christian Andersen, not far from the main road."

"Romain mentioned something about this when I saw him," Jonas said matter-of-factly.

"Avilda discovered the body, and knowing she's the biggest gossip in Odense I'd say the news is spreading quickly, not to mention the body is that of Elsbet Sørensen, the daughter of the wealthiest family in central Denmark," Waage said, ignoring Jonas.

"A murder?" the stranger asked.

"Not sure, Simon. She was hanged so it may be a suicide."

"But you mentioned she came from a wealthy family?"

"Yes. Everyone knows the Sørensen's. Personal friends of mine, awful tragedy really. Elsbet was in her early twenties, bright, an educator at a boarding school nearby. We can't rule out suicide, but I want to treat this as a murder" Waage said, and Jonas thought to himself about how arrogant Waage was sounding now that he spoke in English.

"Have the parents been notified?" Jonas asked.

"Yes, and that's where I need you two. Jonas, Simon is our newest member of the force. As you know, Ejnar is away at the moment and we don't know when he'll be back. Romain is on leave as of thirty minutes ago, and I hired Simon to come and work here. Luckily for us, he starts today. He used to work for the central London police force, so he knows his way around a crime scene" Waage laughed, then after seeing Simon's rather serious face, continued. "Since this is a high profile case we need someone like Simon. He's still learning Danish, so you'll help him there. You're a traffic cop, so don't think you're taking the lead on this one. You haven't worked a murder in… what is it? Twenty years? Anyway, listen to Simon. I don't want to hear you trying to be the hero here." Jonas felt his cheeks turn pink and slumped back into the seat.

"Let's get going, then," Simon said, rising from his chair.

Jonas reluctantly nodded and stood up, following Simon out the door and ignoring Waage's reluctant invitation to shake his hand.

Despite the situation, Jonas took small satisfaction in the fact that now he had been assigned his first 'proper' case in some years, even though the one who handed it to him didn't seem particularly thrilled about it. Only last week he was talking to Romain, who had been involved in a stolen car pursuit through the town, which had ended fatally on the thief's part. This, in turn, put his colleague in the position of being the bearer of bad news to the family and subsequently a key witness for other occupants of the police cars involved.

And to top off his week of triumphs, Romain had stopped and helped a local farmer whose sheep had become wedged between some fencing, not a crime by any accounts but Romain had seemed to single-handedly manage to confirm with victory his all round status of the local policeman good guy who not only could catch criminals and save victims, but also understood the vital importance of a farmer's livelihood out in the countryside and rescue the very animal who was going to put food on the table and pay the farmer's mortgage.

A local hero, smarmy bastard, thought Jonas. He wasn't even fully Danish. He had thought about Romain during the meeting with Waage – surely Waage had the power to pull Romain in from holiday. He couldn't help but feel paranoid that perhaps Waage was setting him up, but he knew he had to dismiss such a thought as it would only hinder the case.

10

London, United Kingdom

Michael had been quick to leave the house in the morning, he had avoided any in-depth conversation with Sanne over their usual early morning cup of coffee and he had even managed to leave a note rather than telling her face to face that he would be late home again. Michael had owed it to a meeting but wasn't sure how long this could go on for.

He had not gone into work for the day but instead had spent most of the morning trying to get his head together, working out where he should go from here.

He decided with himself, after a couple of beers at a pub in Greenwich, that he would head over to the other side of town tonight and hoped he would be allowed into an underground Poker game. Given the heads up about it through a contact in the local Polish community, Michael knew that this was his only hope.

The fear and guilt seemed to be taking over his life and he rationed with himself that if he could only pay back the money then at least he was repenting in some way.

"Bloody Catholic upbringing" he cursed to himself as the guilt started to build up again inside his mind.

Realising that he had spoken out loud whilst on the tube, Michael stood up and took the decision to walk the next few stops.

As soon as he exited the tube station his phone buzzed again illustrating to him that the threat level had just been raised.

11

Odense, Denmark

News of the wealthy girl who hung herself in town had spread quickly as one news site after another picked up the story, every one sure to mention that it was Elsbet Sørensen who had been found. Some of the more right-wing channels were leaning towards murder, whereas the left leaning stations had made claims that every wealthy girl struggles just like everyday people and that suicide isn't uncommon in the rich.

Both sides were now waiting in anticipation outside the grand gates that surrounded the mansion belonging to the Sørensen home. Cameras and microphones at the ready, they were anxious to be the station with the first glimpse of the grieving parents.

It was going to be a sunny day as if the weather had decided that the death of one of the townspeople was no reason for dropping a few grey clouds into the otherwise perfectly blue autumn sky, untroubled by a breath of wind.

Simon and Jonas drove up to the gate and were greeted with microphones hitting the windscreen, but were able to get clearance into the home without much hassle. Simon only wondered how long it would take them to write his name online, and for Sanne to find it.

As Simon and Jonas pulled up at the rather grand, double-fronted house on a private road just out of Odense, Simon couldn't help but wonder how people earned their money as they approached the white-clad home, which looked strikingly different from a typical Danish home – it almost looked a little too British for Denmark. The long, slightly wavy driveway had been worked out perfectly to show off every rockery and water feature, and view. The white, double-storey home stood out and while it was known as one of the first major homesteads around Odense, it had been kept alive well into the 21st century with its various modern add-ons.

As Jonas pulled up the car he turned off the engine and sighed. His beat-up BMW from the eighties looked incredibly out of date next to the brand new Mercedes and the Jaguar that accompanied it. Simon hesitated about leaving the car and instead waited for Jonas to make the first move.

"How do you want to do this?" Jonas asked, sure to put extra effort into the deep exhale it took before opening his mouth, as though to signal he was defeated already.

"We need to rule out that it was a suicide," Simon said, checking his phone. Sanne hadn't messaged him, and while Simon thought he should be relieved, he couldn't help but feel hearing nothing was worse than being hassled.

"You don't think it was a suicide?" Jonas asked.

"You do?"

"Well, she ended up on that lamp post somehow. A girl from a family such as this, I can't imagine all the secrets they were hiding. I've heard rumours…"

"Forget those rumours" Simon opened the door and stepped out into the front driveway. He watched as the front door opened, a man looking out from behind its grandeur. He heard Jonas stumble out of the car and lock the door with his key, and with that the two men headed towards the front door.

"Are you the detective?" the man said, hiding behind the door.

"Yes. Do you speak English?" Simon responded. The man nodded. "Good. I'm Simon Weller, the detective assigned this case. This is my assistant, Jonas Norgaard" he added, somewhat disappointed he couldn't see the look on Jonas' face as he had stressed the word 'assistant'.

"Ah, yes. Waage mentioned he was sending you. I'm Martin Sørensen. My wife is inside waiting for us." The man opened the door wide now and motioned for the men to come in. Martin was a simple looking man. A pair of trendy circular glasses sat on the edge of his nose, and his short brown hair was carefully combed into a prominent side part. His rather large ears stuck out on either side of his head and seemed to draw attention to his tightly buttoned shirt and matching tie. There was nothing particularly impressive about his appearance, in fact, many would consider him quite an ugly man. But it seems wealth was able to change that around, and his styling made every attempt to hide his actual appearance. He was tall, as were most Danish men. His slender frame gave off a certain hint of dominance, and while it didn't affect Simon much he could see Jonas had slumped his soldiers in compliance.

Martin motioned the two men through the hallway, which was lined with certificates, awards and medals. A large black coat hanger stood beside the door, as well as a screen showing nine different angles of the front yard, driveway, and awaiting press on the other side of the gate. The checker floorboard would be considered ugly in any other room, but here it seemed the stylist had made it work. Most of the furniture was either white or black, and a large crystal chandelier hung above the entrance. Everything was spotless, as though it was an art installation rather than a home. There were no signs that people actually lived here; no coats on the floor, socks in odd places or dirty umbrellas hanging by the door. Vibeke would've hated a house so clean, Simon thought to himself. She liked objects that didn't match; things with personality. This house was devoid of a personality.

Martin led the men into a sitting room. Sitting on one of three large white sofas was a woman, slender and delicately waiting for the men. Simon thought about how much this woman looked like the body that had been discovered before. Realising this was the mother, Emilia, Simon was taken aback by how she presented herself. She stood up to greet the men, and she was exquisitely beautiful. She was clearly at least ten years younger than Martin, tall, slim and with white blonde hair tied back, pulling her face back with it. Her large blue eyes were cold but mesmerising, and her tight black dress echoed both sophistication and a sort of sexual playfulness. What struck Simon most was the fact the woman didn't look sad. Her cheeks weren't the puffy red Simon had gotten used to seeing from Sanne over the week following Vibeke's death. The woman's eyes weren't bloodshot and her clothes weren't randomly selected. Everything about her appearance was planned, and maybe the same carried to her emotion. Her nose stuck up in the air and her hand that reached out to shake his seemed quick to pull back after the pleasantries were exchanged. Simon hadn't crossed a woman like this in Denmark before.

"I didn't realise the Funen Police were taking this so seriously," Emilia said, sitting back into her sofa, sure to make sure her back was tightly upright. She looked Simon up and down, and her nose sniffed in slight disgust, though unimpressed by Simon's appearance.

"What do you mean?" Simon said, sitting next to Jonas across from her. Martin joined his wife and put his arm around her. She didn't respond to the gesture.

"Sending a British detective in. I'm glad to see it's been taken so seriously" she said. Simon wanted to correct her but was interrupted in thought by Jonas.

"Birgitte and I are so sorry to hear what happened," Jonas said. Emilia smiled and bowed her head.

"Thank you" she responded, in a line, she had rehearsed well before. Jonas smiled and sat back into the sofa. Simon wondered if Emilia knew Jonas at all, or if she was just being polite.

"What happened is dreadful. Who could do this to our daughter?" Martin said, visibly more upset than his wife.

"That's what we are trying to work out. Do you have any reason to believe someone was after her?" Simon said.

"She was a prominent member within the community. Everyone knew our Elsbet" Emilia smiled.

"Your English is very good," Simon stated, watching Emilia's face light up as he said it. The first sign of an uncontrolled emotion.

"Thank you. We travel a lot. Both Martin and I studied in Oxford and Cambridge respectfully, and we travel to New York once every three months. We were actually there last month. Elsbet didn't come on that trip, she was starting her new job" Emilia said.

"Was it stressful for her? I can imagine for someone just finished studying a new job can be daunting" Simon responded.

"Oh, well I suppose so" Emilia answered briefly.

"Was she depressed?" Jonas blurted out.

"What are you saying? You think she killed herself?" Martin said.

"You think she killed herself" Emilia gasped.

"Not necessarily, we just need to check everything," Simon said, trying to subdue the situation. Emilia ignored him.

"My daughter was beautiful, well-loved and had everything she could ask for. She was happy" Emilia exclaimed.

"I don't doubt that. I apologise." Jonas said, slouching back into his seat.

"When did you last hear from her?" Simon said, changing the topic.

"Well, we were supposed to dine together last night. Martin and I were over at the Albrectsens. Their son was visiting from Oxford and we had encouraged Elsbet to come with us. He's a lovely young man and, well, we thought he would be a good match. She refused, of course. Was locked up in her room. We were going to meet her here after our visit to talk to her about how she'd been acting lately" Emilia said.

"How she'd been acting lately?" Simon repeated.

"Yes." Emilia said, turning to Simon now with her nose back in the air. "She had been acting very quiet, I suppose."

"Was she dating anybody?"

"No. She seldom has a boyfriend. Actually, she dated this boy in Sweden while she was there finishing her studies." Emilia said.

"What can you tell us about him?"

"Not much. Boys always liked Elsbet. She's had boys chasing her since she was little. She's always been less than interested, though" Emilia could see that Simon was rolling his eyes, so she changed the topic. "She dated the Swede for about a year, but broke up when she came home."

"Yes, I remember now. She told me this boy was coming to Odense and wanted to see her" Martin added. Simon could feel Jonas looking at him in shock.

"Do you have a name for this ex-boyfriend?" Simon asked, ignoring Jonas.

"Oh, it was this ugly name. Hektor" Emilia said.

"And what can you tell us about him? Have you met him?" Simon asked.

"We never went to Sweden. She never brought him here. She was so secretive" Emilia scoffed.

"No surname? No nothing?" Simon said.

"Well, it's probably written in her journal. She wrote everything in there"

"Can I see it?"

"I don't see why not. Come, I'll take you to her room" Emilia said, standing up. Simon did so obediently and followed her up the main staircase and down a long hall that was lined of various parties, celebrities, and of course included in the photos either Emilia and Martin or Elsbet. He studied Elsbet's face. She was a beautiful girl, not a feature out of place. But he couldn't help but sense sadness in her appearance. Her face reminded him of Sanne. He wondered how she was. But his headache from his night of wine had taken over his thoughts and he wanted nothing more to sit back down.

Emilia took Simon to the end room and opened the door. "She kept a messy room" she added. Simon nodded, unsure of what to say. He was struggling with grief himself and knew what it was like to hear other say the wrong thing, so he thought it would be best to keep quiet.

He studied the room. In the centre was a large bed that was neatly tucked into place. Her closet was its own room and there was an en-suite next to it. Overlooking the back garden was a balcony that was filled with potted plants. Simon turned to her study corner, which looked as though it was out of place. While everything else was neatly kept like a display room, her bookshelves were packed to the brim with papers, and her desk had piles of papers nudged around a large iMac. Clothes and food packets sat around the desk. He approached it and began to sift through the papers.

"There's a lot here about a school?" Simon questioned, looking at images of an old brick building. He couldn't make out the words but seeing 'skole' over and over led him to the reasonable conclusion.

"Yes, she worked at one." Emilia said, almost sarcastically.

"She has a lot here about a school," He said, flicking through the papers.

"She takes her job seriously. Now, do you need me to stay here? It's just bringing back so many memories" she said dramatically.

"No, no. I'll look around. Thanks" Simon said. Emilia left and Simon shifted through the papers. He couldn't understand much of it and was hoping he'd find HEKTOR written under an image of a man. That was the only way he was going to get through this case. He regretted moving to Denmark. It was clear he wasn't ready. Sanne was right, he should've stayed in London.

He spent several minutes shifting through the papers. Most of it involved a school, but there were the occasional names circled. None of them made sense to Simon. He reached for a brown leather journal that sat under a pile of newspapers. It was tattered and various post-it notes were sticking out from the side. He opened to one page and felt as though he had struck gold.

It was an image of Hektor and Elsbet. Or so it said underneath. They were on a farm. The caption "Skåne. 14/08/2012. Hektor elsker Elsbet" was easy enough for Simon to read. He looked at Hektor. He towered over Elsbet, and he was long and thin. He had combed blond hair and heavily tanned skin, as though he had been outdoors every day. He looked at Elsbet. Something about her face reminded him of all the photos out in the hallway. Is this how she carried herself through life?

Was she happy with Hektor, or was she just as uncomfortable there? He bookmarked the page and kept flicking through.

Feeling his head throbbing, he decided to go back to Jonas and tell him the news. As he was putting the journal away, a photo fell out. Simon sighed and bent over to collect it, blood rushing to his head and causing his vision to go blurry. He groaned and picked up the photo. Looking at it, his eyes widened.

In the photo was a beautiful young girl. She was beautiful and her smile beamed through the image.

She was Vibeke.

12

Odense, Denmark

Simon didn't remember the journey from Elsbet's house back to the station. He felt dizzy; everything around him seemed so unfamiliar and he was taken aback by what he had seen in her bedroom. He had come to Odense to move on with his life, seek closure and try to make everything worth living for once again. But she was with him. Everywhere. He could feel the presence of the figure who had followed him throughout his dreams. Taunting him with every move.

He felt the photograph burning in his coat pocket. He had taken the diary from her bedroom, that he remembered. He hadn't told Jonas, who he could now see sitting across from him flicking through papers. He hadn't told anyone, in fact. He was growing concerned that he had just taken the most crucial piece of evidence with him. Simon felt cold. He was going to be fired before he solved his first case. Showing it to Jonas would only harm the dominant appearance he had created for himself. Everyone was right. Sanne, Jonas. He shouldn't be here. He wasn't cut out to be a detective in Denmark.

"This guy sure doesn't back down" Simon heard Jonas say, adding a hefty belly laugh. Simon looked up from his daze.

"Sorry?" he said, almost annoyed. Jonas looked confused and the smile left his face quickly.

"The phone? You know, Elsbet's phone?" Jonas said, almost doubting himself.

"Where did you get that?" Jonas looked Simon up and down.

"From her parents. Simon, you were there"

"Oh, right," Simon said, and looked back down at the pile of papers in front of him. Images of the crime scene. Reports from officers that were written out in Danish. He pretended to read them.

"You aren't going to ask what the messages are?" Jonas said, holding the phone in his hand.

"Oh, sorry. What are they? Anything of use?" Simon said. Jonas sighed and started pressing buttons, making muttering sounds regarding how technology was difficult these days.

"Here. This Hektor character. It does seem like they dated. He's sending her messages asking her to meet with him, but she's refusing. Saying she's working on something" Jonas said, reading the screen in front of him.

"You think he's the guy?"

"Well, what do you think? You're the higher up here"

"Yes, but I can't read the messages. What feel do you get from him? Does he sound dangerous?" Simon realised his tone had become sarcastic, but luckily Jonas hadn't picked up on it. He saw Jonas' face turn red at the realisation it was on his shoulders. Jonas hadn't taken such a large responsibility in a case in decades. He read through the messages some more as Simon watched him.

"He's in Odense. Four days ago he told her he was taking the train to Odense to come and see her. She refused, saying she was busy working and that they were finished. He seems persistent, though" Jonas said, placing the phone down.

"Does it say where he's staying?" Simon added.

"He said he was staying in a rented apartment in the centre of town. We should go straight there" Jonas said, almost asking it as a question. He stood up and placed his Helly Hansen coat over his khaki coat. The outfit combination wasn't the latest trend, but here in Denmark, it was all about practicality. Simon had always liked that.

"Yes, alright then." Simon said, throwing the pile of papers into the centre of the table. He knew he hadn't fooled Jonas with his remark;

Jonas was clearly aware that Simon couldn't read the language.

"You didn't tell me if you found anything in Elsbet's room," Jonas said as Simon was putting on his rain jacket. He felt the diary in his coat pocket burning.

"What?" he asked, completely dumbfounded. Jonas rolled his eyes.

"Are you okay? You seem a little" Jonas paused, "out of it."

"I'm fine. I didn't hear you"

"Right. Never mind, then" Jonas said, leaving the room.

13

Odense, Denmark

Simon and Jonas pulled up in front of a fairly uninspiring block of apartments. Cold and brutal in their appearance, the rectangular brick building was devoid of any character. Over the years the Danish government had harshened the landscape and Simon wondered why such a nice city had made these awful choices in the eighties.

He suddenly felt like it was Vibeke talking all over again. She always criticised the series of buildings Odense had built when trying to modernise itself.

Jonas pulled up in front of the building and read an address he had scribbled on a post-it note.

"We're just going to ask him a few questions," Simon said as Jonas put the paper back into his pocket.

"It's obvious he did it, too many things are pointing in his direction. Let's take him into the station, charge him and move on with our lives" Jonas said, dismissing the British detective.

"You may want to be finished with case, but we can't just go and arrest whoever we find first" Simon responded.

"Well, each to their own." Jonas muttered. The two men sat in silence, waiting for the other to make a move.

"Come on, let's go find this Hektor" Simon finally said, opening the car door. Jonas followed silently and the two men walked over to the intercom.

"You sure this is the place?" Simon said, looking around the front garden. Jonas pressed a button that said "Helen" with a smiley face next to it and listened as it rang.

"Hello?" the bubbly voice buzzed through from the intercom.

"Hello. I am looking for a man named Hektor. Is he here?" Jonas responded.

"Um, how did you know someone was staying here?"

"We have reason to believe a young Swedish man named Hektor is currently renting a room in your apartment. May we come up? We need to speak to him."

"Well, he's not here. Are you the police?"

"Yes. Now let us in" Silence fell from the other end and Simon looked at Jonas, who looked visibly flustered. His cheeks had turned pink and sweat was starting to form on his brow. Simon watched Jonas wipe the sweat away with his jacket, as though completely unaware that Simon was standing right next to him.

"Um, okay. Yes. Second floor, first on the right" she responded, and the door next to them clicked open. Walking into the doorway, the building greeted them with a rush of modernity, something clearly not visible from the outside. The wooden floorboards had been recently polished and the grey walls screamed Scandinavian design. The staircase itself looked slightly more worn but was lined with pop art prints of various objects. Potted plants lined the railing.

"You don't want to take the lift?" Simon said as he noticed Jonas groaning at the stairs.

"Do you see a lift?" Jonas snapped back. Simon looked around and realised that the building didn't have one. Perhaps the people who lived here were too cool to use an elevator. Simon muttered an apology but it seemed to go unnoticed to Jonas, who had already started his ascent.

The two men arrived at the apartment and were instantly greeted by a young girl, standing in the doorway with her arms crossed. Her long, blonde hair was plaited on either side and her bright blue eyes expressed concern. She was wearing rather tight clothes and Simon could hear some music coming from her apartment. She looked both Simon and Jonas up and down before speaking to them.

"You don't look like the police," she said, observing the two men. Jonas sighed and pulled out his badge, accidentally pulling some receipts with it. The young girl smirked while she watched him pick the receipts off her couch.

"Look, it's not illegal to rent out a bedroom," she said, turning to Simon and ignoring Jonas, who was fumbling to place his badge back into his pocket.

"We are looking for Hektor" Jonas stuttered as he pulled out his notebook.

"Well, he's not here at the moment. I haven't seen him all day. He is going back to Sweden tomorrow so he'll have to come and get his stuff at some point. I'll let him know you stopped by" Helen pouted.

"Helen, we believe Hektor is involved in a crime. May we please see the room he's currently renting?" Simon said, his English causing Helen to look at him in disbelief. Simon ignored the sigh that Jonas had let out and looked at Helen. Her blue eyes were now tearing up and her shoulders released themselves from the intimidating pose she was trying to convey.

"What? Oh, my god. You're saying he killed someone? Wait, is that the news? Elsbet? He killed Elsbet?" Helen responded in Danish. She covered her mouth in shock.

"You knew Elsbet?" Simon said. Helen nodded her head and stood to the side.

"Come in, we can talk about it inside. I don't want the neighbours listening" Helen said. Simon and Jonas stepped into her apartment, which was richly decorated as though it had come straight out of a magazine spread. Everything was either white, grey or pink, and hanging from the entrance hall was a beautiful lime green bicycle. A particularly flowery scent spread throughout the apartment, and

Simon particularly marvelled at the stainless steel kitchen that was remarkably clean for a young girl.

"Is this your apartment?" Simon asked. Helen sat on the grey armchair and crossed her legs. She looked around at her apartment briefly before glaring at Jonas as he slumped down on the sofa, causing it to creak. Simon pulled up a chair from the dining table and sat across from Helen. He watched her – she couldn't have been much older than Sanne when Sanne had her first child. Sanne had been similar to Helen – rebellious, desperate to portray an image. Michael had settled her down and Simon almost mourned for the Sanne that used to be. She had given up the life she had for a family. She could've been like Helen: sitting in a lavish apartment enjoying her younger years.

"Yes. I'm renting out the room to help with the renovations." She responded.

"So how do you know Elsbet?" Jonas interrupted, clearly frustrated.

"Well, we went to school together. Everyone knows her parents, of course. Oh my god! You don't think I had anything to do with this? I haven't seen Hektor. He didn't tell me anything. Oh my god" Helen said, gasping and placing her hands over her cheeks. Tears formed in her eyes and her head collapsed into her hands.

"We aren't saying you did anything. Can you tell us about Elsbet first? What was she like? You were friends?" Simon asked. Helen looked up and Simon questioned whether or not her tears were real. Helen let out a brief laugh before heading to the bookcase that sat next to her flat screen. It was packed with various books, most of which seemed to be biology textbooks. Some had labels that resembled the University of Southern Denmark logo. She pulled out a rather large book, flicked it open to a particular page and showed it to Simon. It was a class photograph. She placed her finger onto a face and then went back to her armchair.

"That's Elsbet. We weren't really friends – she was quiet and weird. My parents are friends with her parents so when we were kids they'd try to make us socialise. But she was so strange. She refused to come to parties in upper secondary and I gave up. Last I heard she went to Sweden to study. Like Swede's are going to be better for her. She was really beautiful, though. She always had the nicest things. I liked going to her house just to marvel at everything she had. Have you ever seen a twelve-year-old with a Chanel purse? She once gave me a Skagen watch just for my birthday. Obviously, her parents picked it out, but I was only eight. The watch had diamonds! Diamonds! I think I still have it somewhere…"

"You do know that Hektor was in a relationship with Elsbet?" Jonas interrupted, and Simon was almost thankful for his poor behaviour this time. Maybe he should be glad Sanne didn't end up like this after all. Helen's face dropped as she took in the news.

"What? No way. Hektor is… well. I didn't think she'd ever find someone. Wait, he's here to visit her?" Simon could almost see her brain processing the information she was hearing and decided to change the conversation.

"Do you know where he is? We really need to find him?"

"No, I haven't seen him in… well since he checked in. I'm rarely home these days. I haven't seen or heard him."

"So you don't know if he's here now?"

"It… it doesn't feel like he's here. I'd know, right?" Simon and Jonas looked at each other.

"Can we please see the bedroom he's renting?" Jonas asked.

"Oh my god, you think he's here!" she said, letting out a gasp. Simon watched her as her face dropped and he started to see some true emotion as she became scared. She pointed to a door in the back corner of the apartment.

14
Odense, Denmark

Simon and Jonas were standing either side of a door, ready to open it. Across the room, the apartment's owner watched in shock. Simon could hear her muttering a mixture of 'oh my god!' and profanities, but ignored her dramatic reaction. Could the case be this easy? Part of him hoped so. It would certainly look good to the police station if he was able to solve a large murder case in only a couple days. On the other hand, he was almost hoping there'd be more of a chase. He needed to keep himself busy, and almost wanted to justify stealing the book from Elsbet's room.

Questions circled through Simon's head as Jonas knocked on the door. After no response, Jonas went to turn the knob. He proceeded to swing the door open and step into the room, shouting 'police!' as though he'd watched one too many crime dramas. Simon followed, immediately recognising the room was empty. Somewhat glad, he looked over to the bed, which was unkempt and had some shirts scattered over the top. A small suitcase sat on top of a desk and was wide open. Simon went over to it and flicked through the contents. Nothing seemed out of the ordinary, so after a quick search, the two returned to Helen.

"We're going to need his phone number, email address, photo, everything," Jonas said, clearly frustrated.

"He wasn't there?" she said desperately.

"Are you going to do what I said or just sit there?" Jonas said. Simon looked at him and tried to motion at him to back down, but Jonas was now ignoring him.

"I… I'll go print everything I have." Helen said. Simon nodded and she went over to another door on the other end of the apartment. While the two men waited, Jonas took various notes in his notebook and ignored Simon's presence. Simon decided to break the silence.

"So what do you think?" Simon asked as Jonas finished his note taking.

"It's simple, isn't it? We take her in, hold her until we find Hektor. Arrest the both of them" Jonas said.

"What? She clearly has nothing to do with it"

"You just think this is all one big coincidence, then? Ex-boyfriend comes and stays with a girl who knew Elsbet, and then Elsbet is found dead with the ex now missing. I'd say Helen is trying to cover for him"

"You're crazy. Look at her; she doesn't know what's going on. Let's just get his number and leave" Simon said almost desperately. With that, Helen came from her bedroom with a pile of paperwork. She sat down and placed it on the coffee table. She began to flick through the pages at Simon.

"This is his phone number and email address. Oh, and his home address. This is what he has to send to me when he rents the room. This here is his Facebook page – with his profile picture. I've also printed out his posts. He writes about coming to Denmark here" she said, pointing at a Swedish status. Simon nodded, and Helen looked at him with a grin.

"You don't speak Swedish either? He says that he's coming to Denmark to make things right. And in this post, it shows him out at a club here in Odense. It's popular with university students. The photographer lets you tag yourself in the photos, so he must've tagged himself. Or someone else. Anyway, that's all I know about him. I hope this helps" she said, pushing the papers towards Simon, who collected them and flicked through them.

"Thanks, Helen. We'll be in touch if we need anything else. Call us straight away if he returns." Helen nodded and leant back in her armchair, fear clearly marked on her face.

*

The rest of the day had been spent at the station. Simon and Jonas looked through his social media history as far back as it went. They found photos of Hektor and Elsbet together, happily enjoying Stockholm's museums, the Swedish countryside and even a trip to Finland the two took together. Hektor hadn't made any posts in Denmark except for the photo he had been taken in, and when Jonas called the club they had told him bluntly that they get hundreds of kids like him and they wouldn't remember a specific face. Besides having police keeping an eye out in Odense, there wasn't much that could be done. They had hit a dead end. Hoping that they would get a call from Helen that he would return, the two men decided to call it a day and headed home. Simon chose to walk; he felt the fresh autumn air was refreshing after a long day. Jonas was proving to be a difficult man to work with and Simon hoped it wouldn't become a regular occurrence. His lack of the language was also making him question his own intentions, and he was trying to find the right way to admit defeat to Sanne. Perhaps even finally sell the house and head back to England. That thought upset him – he couldn't imagine himself surrounded by the family he had left. While he loved his children and his grandchildren, he didn't see himself as the family man without Vibeke. Sanne was busy with her life and Thomas had always been hard to approach. Vibeke was the common factor that brought everyone together and calmed everyone. Simon always seemed to be the one questioning his children's choices and having them resent him at times. He couldn't go home and resume this role. He had to stay here; almost a punishment for decades of bad parenting.

Returning home, he threw his coat onto the living room floor and heard the book thud against the floor. Sitting back in his armchair, he pulled it out of the pocket and opened to the page of Vibeke. The photo was blurred and Simon only now realised it was actually hard to see the girl he believed to be his wife. She resembled the girl he met in the bar; long, blonde hair reaching down her back with a rag turned into a headband in order to keep it out of her face. She was wearing an apron but that was all Simon could make out. He looked at it and longed for it to be her. He decided to flick through the other pages to see why his wife was in the diary, but the pages contained almost nothing but text and the Danish scribbles grew frustrating. He turned back to the image and doubted now whether or not it was her.

Angry, he threw the diary across the room. Thoughts were starting to come back into his head. He saw her in the kitchen, now. Preparing her famous homemade bread. She looked over towards him and smiled. Simon reached for the wine bottle he had picked up from Duty-Free and opened it. He wasn't going to start remembering, not yet.

15

London, United Kingdom

London was enjoying a particularly sunny day for late October. The air was as fresh and clear as it could be in the city, and workers were making use of this dry day by flocking to Regent's Park to have their lunch. Along from Chiltern Street was an older building which had recently been renovated. The stone bricks now looked contemporary and gave an overall feeling of power, and the minimalistic sign above it showed that they regarded themselves to the highest extent. Peckington Insurers were the next big 'up-and-comers' within Central London, and they had spent their success on a new façade and a new identity. A business that for seventy years had prided itself on its family-like feel, its new status as one of the leading insurance firms had put pressure on the company to stay relevant, but they had always believed it was important to do it with family charm.

Thomas couldn't concentrate on his work. Something had been bothering him for a while, but for some reason, it was now giving him the unsettling feeling that something was very wrong. He couldn't help but feel all the signs were there of some sort of betrayal. He stared out of the window and tried to connect the dots.

When Michael had married Sanne, the head of the company, Nigel Taylor, had been quite overjoyed at the prospect of having such a close-knit family amongst colleagues and thus feeding into this traditional ideal. Nigel was an endearing man; it was his father Peter who had started the company and Nigel had carried on this warm tradition. A man in his early to mid-forties, he looked considerably younger, which Thomas had always put down to the constant smile

Nigel wore, as well as the many hours he spent in the gym around his busy work schedule. Thomas remembered clearly Nigel patting him on the back and congratulating him on the news of the addition to the family, both at home and at work, but for Thomas that notion was best left in the history books: he and Michael were only classed as family through marriage, and as the months went on, Thomas felt less and less like Michael was his brother-in-law. On several occasions, Thomas had overheard Michael acting strangely. Whilst Thomas often poured himself into his work the moment he entered the office which looked onto the city park in Plaistow, he had always kept an eye on Michael whenever he could, since he had married his sister: a kind of paternal instinct Thomas felt his father had sometimes unwittingly lacked, due to the next big case at work.

He had introduced his sister and Michael at a work function. The invitation had said to bring a date and, as Thomas didn't know many other women well enough to invite them along, inviting his sister gave both him and her a laugh, as well as another reason to spend some time together. Michael had instantly charmed her. Thomas hadn't paid much attention to this man around the office before, and when he saw how happy his sister was he dismissed it as nothing more than a bit of flirting. A year later, they were married and Thomas felt as though he had already lost his relationship with her as Michael was desperate to start a family of their own, and Sanne was eager to please. Thomas felt Sanne had married Michael to create some kind of happy ending to her rather wild teenage years. It was as if by writing new chapters she could erase the old ones. But deep down Thomas knew that Sanne still had her old fighting spirit, it had just kind of been diluted since meeting Michael. He had always felt as though Sanne was giving up all intelligence she had. While she had been a party girl during high school, Thomas could see how wonderfully creative she was, particularly with drawing and painting. He had tried to get her to attend classes, but her rebellious attitude had usually caused all plans to fall through. Now, with a marriage under her belt, Sanne could resign herself to the fact that her only job herself was to be a stay-at-home mother, and Thomas was always unsure if that was what she really enjoyed.

Thomas actually adored being an uncle and loved every bit of Lucy and Sam. Lucy, the younger, looked very much like his mother, Vibeke, and had a certain Danish look to her. Sam was a quieter character, and sometimes Thomas despaired at how Michael held him back from being a little boy. He would stop Sam from climbing trees, getting muddy or speeding around on his bike, because Michael had not done that as a boy. Instead, Michael tried to make his son more like him: studying mathematics. Sam had a natural intelligence, but he always envied the boys who could go and play football on their weekends while he was stuck inside being guided through a textbook by his financial father. Little did Michael know that when he went up to their other branch in Manchester on occasional weekends, Sanne would allow Thomas to come over and take Sam out for a few hours to go fishing, climb a tree, ride his bike down hills and just generally let go. Thomas would always deliver a very happy boy back home, muddy and with a few cuts, but it was worth it.

While Thomas knew his place now in Sanne's life, he couldn't help but keep a watchful eye out. And he always felt there was another side to Michael, not just this overcautious boring insurance family man that he liked to portray. This feeling was confirmed in Michael's eyes when he overheard at work, about two weeks after Vibeke had passed away, a brief phone call in which Michael was asking when the krone would arrive. Thomas had only just gone back to work after the funeral and felt like the first few days were a bit of a blur. But he was still sure of what he had heard. Michael had never bothered to learn Danish but Thomas had picked up the word 'krone' from listening to his mother's stories. Michael never cared for the Danish side of his wife's life, so the mention of the word was definitely odd behaviour.

Two days later when Thomas was leaving the office he saw Michael parked in the car park and, although he couldn't hear what was being said and to whom, he could see that Michael was clearly enraged and very animated on the phone.

When that weekend Michael had gone up to Manchester again and Thomas had called round to collect Sam, he casually asked if Michael was ok and if Sanne was expecting money from Denmark. Sanne didn't know what Thomas was talking about and said he must have misheard the word 'krone'. She was more worried in speaking to Thomas about their dad and how he wasn't coping with Vibeke's death, and Thomas figured it best he play along. He could see in Sanne's eyes that she was close to breaking and more than anything he didn't want this. Vibeke's death had pulled the family apart and true, their dad was disintegrating day by day but Thomas felt this was a natural part of the grieving process. He had found some comfort in talking to a counsellor, but had done this on the quiet. He liked to solve his own problems.

Sanne had mentioned that she and Michael were planning to sell the Danish house, and Thomas thought this was another one of Michael's pushy ideas and just shrugged, saying it was their fathers choice. With that, he picked Sam up and took him out for what ended up being a very successful day of fishing.

The day before Simon left for Denmark, Thomas had been at work making his way to the staff canteen. As he passed one of the filing rooms he heard a familiar voice: what struck Thomas was not the fact that Michael was in a room that he had no business being in, on the phone, but that he was almost whispering as he spoke. Thomas couldn't make out the conversation but he was sure he heard his mother's name mentioned. Michael, though outwardly charming, had never been interested in getting to know Vibeke. He had been interested in Simon's line of work and always looked for opportunities to sit down and discuss socio-political issues and the business side of the police force, but he had never once started a conversation with Vibeke.

When Vibeke died, Michael wasn't at the funeral. Sanne had said he was trapped at work, but this felt not quite right to Thomas as he knew the office would never keep someone from attending the funeral; they were overly kind when it came to taking time off for personal matters. Thomas was beginning to have doubts as to whether Michael was being faithful to Sanne: had he actually meet someone in Denmark the last time they went out? Sanne had commented on how much he had gone off by himself for walks.

Thomas watched the tips of the trees on the street sway against the cool breeze of the London autumn. Michael was a strange guy, but not strange enough to commit something awful. But as far as Thomas was concerned, Michael was up to something and it had something to do with someone in Denmark.

16

Odense, Denmark

With two bottles of wine came a throbbing hangover and Simon didn't entirely remember making it into the police station the next morning. But here he sat at his temporary desk, photos of Elsbet scattered in front of him. The night had brought with it the usual thoughts he had of Vibeke, and when he woke up at 4 am he held his head as he tried to make himself forget everything. He had made it into the office by 6 am, and had been sitting here for almost three hours looking through photographs. Everything blurred together and he instead decided to pretend to be busy, only to stop people talking to him.

Simon hadn't realised, though, that no one had been in the office and it was only after nine o'clock that officers started to enter the building. He ignored their glances as they walked past, and wondered whether or not he had changed out of yesterday's clothes.

It was around nine thirty that Jonas came through the door, coffee and donut in his hands. He sat down across from Simon and looked at his partner.

"Jesus, Simon. Did you go home last night? You look awful" Jonas said, taking a bite out of his doughnut.

"Huh? Oh, right. Bad night's sleep." Simon said, rubbing his head. Jonas picked up the smell of wine that was now coming from Simon's mouth and put his doughnut down, almost put off.

"I see. You didn't notice this note on my desk, then?" Jonas said, showing it to Simon.

"It's in Danish, so no. Didn't bother" Simon said, scratching his head.

"Well, it says they've got Hektor downstairs. Found him drunk in a park and brought him in" Jonas said, almost laughing in disbelief. Simon grabbed the note and noticed a few familiar words, enough to believe him. Standing up, he felt his headache start to throb once more but ignored it as he motioned for Jonas to follow him.

The two men went down to the holding cells and Jonas had a conversation with the young officer on duty. The officer clearly knew Jonas, and the two had a rather friendly chat, the officer even laughing at some of Jonas' jokes. Simon watched in disbelief as the two men exchanged pleasantries; a type of exchange Simon was yet to receive from a Dane.

Walking across the empty floor which seemed rather empty, Simon was reminded of how crowded the London holding cells would be in the morning. Full with prostitutes, alcoholics, drug dealers and petty criminals, he never was a fan of walking through the halls in the morning. The cells in Odense were small – there were only a couple of them, and in one was a drug addict quietly sobbing. The other one held Hektor, who Simon recognised instantly. His blonde styled curls looked greasy and unkempt, and he was sitting with his head in his hands.

"Hektor, you speak English?" Simon asked. Hektor looked up at him. Simon was overcome with a sadness from the boy's eyes; he had clearly been crying and his mouth was trembling. It reminded Simon of the only time he had seen Thomas upset over Vibeke's death. He had accidenty stepped into Thomas's bedroom as Thomas was on the bed crying. Thomas never displayed emotion and had instantly been embarrassed that he had been caught.

"Yes" he said. Jonas unlocked the cell and motioned for Hektor to follow. He obediently did so and the men went into an interview room.

"So, why were you sleeping in a park?" Simon asked. He found himself taking control of the interview, much to Jonas' dismay. Perhaps it was his throbbing headache, but Simon wasn't in the mood to listen to his attempted arrogance.

"I went out last night. I drank a lot. I fell asleep there" Hektor stuttered.

"Any reason you were out drinking?"

"I'm on holiday. I decided to go out and meet people."

"You're Swedish, right?"

"Yes"

"Stockholm?"

"No, I just study there. I'm from Skårby. It's just out of Ystad in Skåne. My parents own a farm there" Hektor said.

"So why did you come for a holiday to Odense?" Hektor looked at Simon. He hesitated to answer and slouched in his chair.

"It was for Elsbet, wasn't it?" Jonas blurted out. Hektor looked at him in shock.

"I... yes. We were going to make our relationship try to work. I wanted to make it work. I loved her." He said, tearing up.

"Loved? So you know she was found dead, then?" Jonas said angrily. Hektor started to cry.

"She killed herself, didn't she? I... I saw it in the papers. She killed herself because of me" he cried.

"What makes you say it was because of you?" Simon asked. Hektor wiped his tears.

"Well... the day she... killed herself. I had gone to visit her. I asked her if we could try and make things work, but she wasn't interested. I begged to make it better. I said I'd move to Odense so she wouldn't have to give up her job. But Elsbet was so... she was so obsessed with her work. She told me to leave, that it was over. That she was busy with something. I tried to stay. I yelled at her. Called her selfish and said she'd never find anyone as good as me."

"Did she get upset?"

"No. Didn't even shed a tear. Told me that I was distracting her and to get out"

"Distracting her from what?"

"Oh, the usual. She was obsessed with research, studying people. She didn't trust anyone. I remember when we first started dating I was in her bedroom and found she had been searching my name on the internet. I confronted her about it and she said she was trying to make sure I wasn't a criminal. I almost broke up with her then but, well…"

"She's rich" Jonas scoffed.

"Sorry?" Hektor asked.

"You stayed with her because of the money. You saw this wealthy girl who is clearly not popular and figured you were the only guy for her. You stayed with her for the money"

"I knew she had money; but it wasn't just about that. She was sweet, smart… she had nice qualities." Hektor's last statement had discouraged Simon, who had been desperate to sympathise with the boy. Perhaps he didn't want Jonas to be right about him, but Simon was hoping Hektor was innocent. Looking at him again, he was wearing expensive clothing and all the photos from his social media showed him to be always very well dressed. "I couldn't see her killing herself, though"

"What makes you think she killed herself?" Simon responded.

"What? You think she was murdered? You think I… look I had nothing to do with her death. After I saw her I went back to Helen's and we went clubbing all night. I woke up around midday yesterday and saw that she was in the papers. I… I didn't expect it. I went and bought some vodka and sat in the park crying and drinking. It's pathetic, but I love her. I loved her."

"Why not go to Helen's then? Why outside?"

"I was embarrassed. Helen and I hooked up, and I didn't want her to see me crying over an ex."

"So you were with Helen all night?" Jonas asked.

"Yes. We drank and partied and then went back to Helen's to hook up." Hektor said, almost proud of himself.

"Did Helen know Elsbet?" Simon asked.

"I… I don't know. It's a small town" Hektor responded briefly.

"We know Helen knew Elsbet. Now the question is whether or not you're lying to us now." Jonas added.

"Alright, okay. Helen showed me these photos of Elsbet. She told me that she and her friends would make fun of Elsbet. They would throw things at her and call her names. I found it funny at the time because I was angry. Not that I'd kill her, just that she'd rejected me. I've never been dumped before. She was so blunt about it…"

"Hektor. You knew Helen didn't like Elsbet?"

"No one liked her. Helen told me that her parents would make her go and play with Elsbet, but she'd steal Elsbet's things."

Jonas and Simon looked at each other. They excused themselves and stood in the hallway. Simon leaned against the wall and avoided eye contact with Jonas, who was now visibly angry.

"Kids these days… Picking on each other, stealing. We're bringing Helen in… I knew she was no good! I want to make an arrest by the end of the day. Good work, Simon. We've done well. Of course, you should've trusted me on this, but let this be a learning curve. Danish youth are nothing but trouble. Killing a girl over a relationship"

"There's the photo of him at the club. We know he was there that night"

"Oh please, it's not hard to leave. They arranged to meet with her and kill her. Didn't her parents say something about how she was meeting with someone? It all makes sense." Jonas said, pulling out his phone. "Arnar, can you bring in Helen Følsgaard from Filosofgangen 70 and bring her to the station?"

"Let's not jump to any conclusions. We'll ask her to confirm what Hektor told us." Simon added. Jonas ignored Simon and smiled to himself as he went to get some lunch.

It took almost two hours before Helen was brought in. She looked much less refined than when Simon and Jonas had visited her the day before. Her mascara had run down her cheeks from crying and she was in a sweater and leggings. Her hair had been tied in a messy bun and she was screaming about wanting a lawyer.

Simon and Jonas had escorted Hektor back to the holding cell and had been waiting for her to arrive. Simon had tried to speak to Jonas about what approach they should take, but Jonas was eager to make the arrest. He wanted the pat on the back and the attention that comes with solving a big case, and he had almost completely forgotten that Simon was, in fact, the one in charge.

Helen looked visibly scared when she sat down in front of Simon and Jonas.

"Hello Helen, good to see you again" Jonas smiled.

"Look, I had nothing to do with Elsbet's death! I haven't seen her in years. I didn't do it!" she shrieked.

"We aren't saying you did. Just tell us everything that happened since Hektor arrived. From the beginning" Simon said.

"Well, I didn't know he was her ex. He booked my room and I didn't know anything about him. He shows up and tells me he's here to find his ex-girlfriend. I didn't care as I was working on an assignment so I brushed it off. Normally I'd ask but I really didn't care. Well, not until he burst into the apartment after visiting her. I was going to tell him off for yelling and causing a scene, but he told me all about her. He told me she'd dumped him and he'd never been dumped before and she didn't even care. I asked who the girl was as Odense is small and I, of course, knew Elsbet right away. We spent a couple hours drinking and making fun of her. Then I suggested we find him a new girl and we went clubbing. We partied and drank and ended up hooking up. When I woke up the next day, a couple hours before you showed up, he had disappeared. I was annoyed because I really liked him and he just up and left. Then you mentioned that he was involved in a crime and I became scared. I panicked"

"Did you leave the club at any point to meet with Elsbet?" Simon asked.

"No, I haven't seen her in years. Like she'd go to a club anyway."

"Did Hektor leave?"

"I… I don't know. We weren't together the whole night. It's really blurry."

"So you bully and steal from this girl your whole life and she's found dead the night you drink and party with her boyfriend? And he was angry with her? You do realise how this sounds?" Jonas said.

"Look, just because I didn't like her doesn't mean I killed her. I was stupid as a kid, of course, I regret it. I have nothing against her – I haven't spoken to her in years."

"Well then do you know if Hektor snuck out to kill her?"

"I… I don't know"

"Well, we'll give you some time to think about it," Jonas said, standing up

"No please don't leave me here. I honestly don't know!"

"We're keeping you here overnight while officers search your apartment," Jonas said. Helen began to sob into her hands.

"It's protocol, Helen. It doesn't mean we think you did it. We are just trying to find out what happened that night." Simon added, trying unsuccessfully to reassure her. The two men left her in there as they went back to their desks.

The officers returned from her apartment in the evening with a small pile of items but nothing that was of use to Simon and Jonas. Frustrated, Simon was ready to tell Jonas he had nothing. He could see Jonas knew it as throughout the day he'd thrown documents, yelled at others to keep quiet and was now rather sweaty. Simon decided it was time to have the dreaded conversation with his partner.

"Jonas, we've been looking all day. There is nothing to show they were there" Simon said. Jonas sighed and looked at Simon.

"We're still waiting to hear from everyone. There's still stuff to come. It's clear they did it – you saw how they acted. Guilty, the both of them"

"I think we need to focus more on what Elsbet was looking into. Her parents and Hektor mentioned she would obsessively look into people. What if she looked into someone a little too much? What if she was meeting that person and they decided to silence her. We need to look into that angle too"

"Not if we have the culprit downstairs. Simon, this is a simple case. It's not some complex detective crime like you're used to. It's a bunch of kids killing over jealousy. It happens"

"Let's just think about it overnight. Come back tomorrow with a fresh idea of everything" Simon said, desperate to leave and head home. He had spent the day thinking about the diary and was now ready to start translating it, despite how slow and painful that process would be. He knew Elsbet had put the answer in there and he desperately needed to find it before Jonas made the arrest.

"Fine by me. We aren't going to get some reports until the morning, anyway. See you tomorrow" and with that Jonas almost stormed out of the building.

17

Odense, Denmark

The trees whistled against the cool evening breeze, a clear sign to Erik Larsson that the cold season was fast approaching. The colours of the garden had long gone. Erik never believed that to be the sign of autumn looking towards winter approaching, but now, as he stood in the empty gardens of Klosterhaven, he felt the silence that the colder months brought to the country.

Erik had finished a day of tending to the herb garden that formed part of the larger garden at Klosterhaven that was accompanied by a grand, old cathedral that had spooked Erik more than the eerie silence caused by the off-peak tourist season. Locals were bored of the garden, so Erik had always looked to the tourists to give the grounds some much-needed attention and praise, but even that only occurred within a select two months. They would come in groups, standing on the path and photographing the stark contrast of the bright roses with the old cathedral, then wander about the gardens and marvel at the herb garden before continuing their journey around Odense. They didn't care for the exotic, rare and beautiful flowers that Erik tended to every day. Rather, they wanted what they had already read on the Internet – the famous cathedral and the famous herb garden.

In this sense, he believed his garden to be his own well-kept secret. He had never felt outgoing about his achievements, and these grounds were another shining example of such a success. When he first started he had hoped his daughter would visit, but she was always so busy with her office job and two young kids to find the time. Erik didn't mind much these days; he had accepted the fact that he was slowly fading away as an old, forgotten man.

Clouds had gathered over the city and Erik could feel rain approaching. It was only 4:30 pm and his role was to remain on the grounds until 6:00 pm, but he had made plans to visit his daughter for dinner and figured no one would come to visit in the rain. He had arrived earlier than usual to make the most of the morning mist and silence. He felt he had earned this opportunity to leave early. Not that he had a boss or someone to answer to – rather, Erik had volunteered at the grounds for the past five years hoping that upon death he would be greeted by God and forgiven for his sins.

He made his way towards his shed and reached into his pocket for the key. The lock creaked open and revealed the contents packing the small space to the brim with old, worn-out tools. He reached out for his bag and pulled out his mobile phone.

"Signe, are you picking me up?" he sighed.

"Oh, you're ready now? Can you take the bus? I'm at the office for another thirty minutes. You can let yourself in. Matt should be home."

"I don't want to be a bother. I'll make my way to your office and we can go together. It's a nice evening."

"No, no. I don't want you walking around in the dark. Not after that girl was murdered. The bus stops right outside the cathedral – just get on and I'll see you soon. Ha det." Signe hung up and Erik found himself once again in silence. Signe had always been overly paranoid – she had got that from her mother. And the constant news cycle of the Sørensen girl's murder was not helping that either. "You're an old man," she had pestered him after the first robbery. "You're a target to these people." But Erik didn't think anything of it – his job was to listen for visitors and he knew that if someone were to sneak in he'd be the first to know it. Or until now.

Erik opened the shed and saw a tall, dark figure admiring the roses. The phone call must've distracted me, Erik thought as he closed and locked the shed behind him.

"Hello, sir. I understand that the sign says we are open until 18:00, but I'm afraid I must close the gardens. May I walk with you out?" Erik said. He rattled his keys lightly, as though a passive-aggressive way to signal the man's exit. The man didn't respond and the familiar silence shone down once again on Erik.

"Sir, can you hear me?" Erik took a step forward.

"Is that a Swedish accent I hear?" A deep voice came from the dark figure. He could see the man more clearly now. He was tall – big, but not obese. He looked as though he had spent his life working outdoors, as the ugly black sweater coat he was wearing could barely contain his large arms and torso. He was wearing a hat, but Erik could make out matted brown hair extruding from the sides.

"Actually, yes. I am from Luleå. But I have lived in Denmark all my adult life," Erik said. He had left the far north city looking for work opportunities – the Swedish Lapland was a slow place to live unless you found the right industry. However, Erik wasn't a working man – rather he had sought Denmark for unique, city-like jobs that would give him large amounts of money and power. While he had found what he was after, he was never able to shake off the accent.

The man fell silent once again. Erik didn't know whether to leave or approach him. The man seemed twice his size and could easily cause harm. He shook these ridiculous thoughts from his mind. He was in a garden next to a cathedral. He was safe. He took a step forward.

"I'm sorry, sir. I must be closing. I have dinner with my daughter." Erik smiled, hoping to find some empathy from the man. "You are welcome to come tomorrow."

"No. This must be today," the man said, turning around. Erik could now see him front on and saw just how large this creature was.

Calling him a man felt wrong. He looked almost satanic, and this caused Erik to start panicking internally. He had served the church loyally for five years as an attempt to better his life. His hustle and bustle city life had brought forward terrible tragedies, and it was not until Erik was old and out of money that he didn't need to commit such terrible things to find happiness. The church had forgiven him, accepted him, and offered him a job at the grounds. However, Erik didn't accept the money. He wanted to volunteer, and five years later he had seen no desire to move on to something else. No matter how often he had tried to fix things, he always felt as though God wasn't watching. While he had caused things that had damaged people, he found himself scared of death as he saw first the grey hair appearing, then the wrinkles, then the sore muscles. His attempts to please this man called God had been unheard. He wasn't a believer, but so many people were that he thought it would work for him. Five years later and here he was in a garden with a devil.

"Please. What have I done?" Erik cried. He could feel the tears forming, but rather than being upset he felt as though he had to bargain with this creature. The devil took a step forward, casting a shadow over Erik's small body and causing him to hunch over. Erik saw the devil place his hand into his ugly sweater and pull out a large, sharp knife.

"But my daughter…" Erik began, holding an arm out in an attempt to plead for mercy. It was then that the devil swung his weapon with such a grace that the whole event was over in less than five seconds. Before Erik had the chance to scream in pain the devil had silenced him. Before Signe had the chance to have dinner with her father in a little over an hour the body of the old man lay abandoned in an old church garden with one less hand. And the devil knew he had taken his vengeance.

As the man calmly walked away from the gardens, paranoia told him that someone was watching him, as he looked at the lady fumbling with her purse as she stood poised on the pavement, he suddenly felt like her eyes were averted towards him.

He had to get home: this city wasn't safe for him anymore.

18

London, United Kingdom

Thomas lay silently in the bedroom of his apartment. It was a small space: inner-city living in London was. Thomas had bought the run-down, 80s-built apartment for the location and not so much the living space. Working full-time at an insurance company had kept Thomas obsessed with his work. What most would find boring he thrived on. Anything to distract him.

He couldn't sleep and knew he had to be up for work in a few hours. But something had caused him to be unable to get rest. Earlier that evening he had phoned Sanne – he received a text message from her a couple of days ago about their father heading over to Denmark. It was only now that he'd bothered to read it. Actually, that was only half-true. He had first glanced at it when she sent it through, but the idea of his father heading over to Denmark had annoyed him to the point that he didn't want to respond.

He had phoned Sanne at home the night before, and instead of being able to talk to his sister, he was stuck with Michael. He had never been interested in Michael's discussions. They came off as arrogant, distant and so self-involved that Thomas was hardly able to get a word in. But this phone conversation had been different.

He had asked straight away for Sanne. No pleasantries or banter. He didn't have the time to care for it. Michael had answered sternly.

"Sanne isn't available, Thomas. She's putting the children to bed. What do you want?" He had sounded nervous, almost unsure of where the conversation was going.

"I want to speak to Sanne. She texted me about Dad and I thought

I should call her." He didn't understand why he had to explain this to Michael. There was a silence over the phone. Michael was thinking.

"I'll get her to phone you back later?" he said slowly, shuffling the phone in his hand.

"Fine, can you get her to call when she's done?" Thomas had said impatiently.

Another long silence.

"Yes, whatever." Michael hung up the phone and Thomas slammed his down.

At first, he likened it to Michael's usual, arrogant behaviour. He grumbled to himself about the rudeness of a man he was supposed to call brother.

As soon as Michael had come off of the phone to Thomas he had shouted up to Sanne that he needed to go to the office for some files and before she was given the chance to object, Michael was already out of the door.

*

The dark narrow stairs took Michael down to the basement level. From where he was standing he couldn't make out the people sitting around the table below. He thought to himself that this must be how they like it. Intimidate the players before the game had even started. The smoke was heavy and further adding to the shielding of the men's faces. As he got closer to the bottom Michael realised how much hearing an alien language was starting to unnerve him.

"Sit!" said a large shaven-headed man. His rolls of fat were clearly visible beneath his shirt although Michael doubted anyone had ever mentioned this faux part to the giant himself.

A cigar held its balance perfectly in his mouth as he spoke, which told him that he had had years of practice.

Wanting to survey the rest of the players around the table without looking nervous, Michael discreetly took off his jacket and placed it on a chair allowing the natural movement to give him a slightly better visual of his comrades.

"Get out money!" said the Polish giant to Michael before he had even had a chance to sit done. How crude Michael thought but complied almost immediately.

"Not enough! We play big here". He shouted through broken English.

"It's all I have."

"The ring with diamonds." came the response from a smaller man sitting on a wooden chair in the corner whilst talking furiously on his phone in Polish.

"I'm sorry." said Michael trying hard to not stutter now at the pure intimidation.

"Ring!" the smaller man repeated and now pointing to clarify his request.

Rubbing his nose between his fingers which Michael often did when nervous he nodded his head in acceptance whilst praying that tonight would finally go his way.

19

Odense, Denmark

Jonas inhaled the smells which surrounded him as he stepped out of his car whilst he pulled back the creaky old gate which had rusted and aged over the years, fencing off his parents' farm to the outside lane. The sun was just beginning to make its appearance and the further he got from Odense, the cleaner the air became and the emptier the streets were. He loved this about the countryside.

As a boy, he used to sit on the gate and wait for his father to finish with his early morning duties before retrieving Jonas from the gate and taking him to school. He longed to come off that gate and one day be a working farmer, helping his parents and working the land of his native country. One morning Jonas' father did just that, and rather than sit on the gate and swing his legs, Jonas was taken by his father's hand and walked down to the pigs where he was given the job to feed them. When his father and he had finished they both wearily walked back up to the farmhouse where Jonas' mum was waiting with an extra-special breakfast for her "working boys", as she liked to call them from that day forward.

His parents were simple folk but not in the derogative sense. They were simple in their life pleasures. They worked hard, were kind and forgiving, and only wanted Jonas to be happy. They had longed for a sibling for Jonas, but it wasn't until Jonas was an adult that he realised that his mother, who had taken to her bed for a few days in the summer of '66, had in fact lost what would have been his little sister. But, true to the woman she was, she was back with a smile on her face baking treats for them the following week.

Jonas knew that his father's dream was for him to take over the farm and Jonas had dreamed that many times also, but unfortunately the world had changed and times were hard for the farmers of Denmark. The day Jonas sat his parents down to tell them he was joining the police force was the day he knew he had broken their hearts, but if there was any chance that Jonas would be able to financially help out with keeping the farm going he felt this was his only option.

Every time Jonas came here he saw how his parents had aged a little more each year and he couldn't bear to think of the day when they might not appear to the sound of his car pulling up to the front.

His mum Pernille was always the first to greet him as his father was normally out somewhere in the yard. Her smile was a warmth which Jonas never saw in Birgitte's face, and it always took him back to his happy childhood.

"Where's Far?" asked Jonas, knowing the answer, but that was the game they liked to play.

"Fixing the boundary fence which is starting to fray. Won't you come in out of the cold, Jonas, and have something to eat? You look like you've lost a few pounds."

Jonas also enjoyed this game from his mum who was forever complimenting him.

"I'm going to help Far first and then we will be down. Birgitte is at the office all weekend so there's plenty of time for me to stay."

With this, Jonas' mum almost gasped with delight and turned on her heels as best she could to go and put some coffee on for her working boys.

The short walk across the farmyard was enough to lead Jonas into a puff which he consciously tried to control as he reached his father. Arto had kept his hefty frame even through age. His skin was weather-worn and his clothes were the same as when Jonas was a boy. He was well liked in the area and had quite a respectful reputation. Arto would have a drink in his local with other farmers but never came home drunk and always showed his mum such respect. Arto was whom Jonas wanted to emulate, but found it hard to act out his ways with his wife Birgitte. She didn't appreciate the kind gestures in the same way his mum did.

"Far, I'm here to help," shouted Jonas, aware of his father's failing hearing.

"Ah what a nice surprise. I've nearly finished, why don't we go and enjoy a coffee and one of your mother's cinnamon buns?" Arto said. Sometimes Jonas felt like his dad still spoke to him as if he was a child. But Jonas quite liked that.

Standing there for the next fifteen minutes, Jonas watched with pride as his father worked on the fence with ease. He was the backbone of Denmark and was who made it great, the way Jonas wanted to keep it.

Picking up his tools, Arto looked at his son and was glad that he had come to visit them. He knew Pernille had been up early baking, in the hope that he would arrive.

As they walked back down, Arto asked Jonas how things were and said someone had mentioned in the pub that there was a killer on the loose. Jonas eased his father's fears and told him that the case wasn't as big as people were making out.

Jonas felt a slight satisfaction that his parents' concern for his well-being had never faltered over the years, but he also didn't want them to worry unnecessarily so he spent well over an hour indulging them with anecdotes and stories which he remembered from his childhood on the farm.

Checking the time, Jonas realised it was getting close to 10 am, and since he had spent so long comforting his parents that Odense was still safe he had forgotten that he was actually supposed to be on this case right now. Digging through his pockets for his phone, he saw that Waage had tried to call him half a dozen times. Dialling the number, Jonas knew he was going to be in trouble.

"Jonas, you were supposed to be in the office over an hour ago," Waage answered.

"Sorry, I'm on my way. The car broke down." Jonas lied. It was the best he could come up with, and he knew any hint of honesty would have him off the case quickly.

"Well don't bother going to the station. Go to Klosterhavn. Someone has been killed" and with that Waage hung up.

*

Simon awoke to find himself on the sofa once more. Confused as to why he was still fully dressed, he cursed to himself about the person he had become.

Sitting up, Simon could instantly feel the three glasses of Brouilly coming back to haunt him and realised that the throbbing he was experiencing was clearly from the bottle of grapes he had succumbed to once again.

Deciding to make some coffee, Simon put in practice a half-hearted attempt to tidy some items from the floor as he got up to head to the kitchen. Rubbing his hands over his chest to try and gain some warmth on what felt like a particularly cold morning, Simon waited for his kettle to alert him that it was ready for him to make some of the black stuff which seemed to keep Denmark on its feet.

As he poured he suddenly became lost in thought as he had a fleeting moment of walking outside in the dark.

Puzzled, Simon walked back into the front room as his head seemed to clear with each sip of caffeine.

Looking on the floor at the rest of the mess which he planned to tidy up after his morning shower, Simon noticed a photo album lying with its middle pages wide open.

Grabbing it for closer inspection, Simon cursed himself almost as immediately as the memory came back.

He had been out for a walk last night, and looking at the photos it was to some of the treasured places he and Vibeke had visited.

Walking round the streets in a drunken state was not a good look for a detective, nor was it safe. Simon suddenly felt very out of control again and hurried to his coat to make sure his wallet was still there. Standing dishevelled in his hallway, he heard his phone start to buzz. Remembering the phone conversation he had with Sanne, at first, he decided to ignore the phone. If it wasn't for the case he would've left it entirely, but knew he it could also possibly be the detective he was working alongside.

"Hello." he said.

"Simon, why aren't you in the office?" Jonas responded brashly.

"I… sorry. I overslept. I'll be there in twenty minutes" Simon said, rubbing his head.

"Go to Klosterhavn. Do you know where that is?"

"Yes"

"Well go there. There's been another murder. Possibly related to Elsbet" and with that Jonas hung up before Simon had the chance to ask further.

Putting his shoes on as he hopped in a hurry on the opposite foot, Simon grabbed a coat and made a run for the park, knowing that he was already cutting it fine with his job.

20

London, United Kingdom

Sanne found herself starting to stir as the very early morning traffic began to flow past her window. Confused at being awake and hearing a different pattern of traffic to what she usually heard, she realised that her sudden jolt from her sleep was the unconscious feeling of the other side of the bed being empty. Michael can't have come home last night, she whispered in her mind.

Getting up from her bed whilst still half asleep Sanne made her way to the stairs and headed on down.

Before she had even reached the bottom she caught sight of her husband lying on the sofa, as her confusion blended in with anger, Sanne shouted out before she could stop herself.

"Where were you last night? Why didn't you come to bed?"

Lifting his head from the cushion Michael looked a wreck.

"Oh my God, you're drunk" she spat.

With tears forming in her eyes Sanne walked closer to him and inspected him further.

"Where's your ring?" she gulped. "My God Michael what have you done?"

"Nothing!" he shouted back although she was now directly in his space.

"Can't I go out with some friends for drinks without you being on my case?" he said.

Taking in what he had said Sanne took a deep breath and lowered her voice as she could feel her emotions trying to take over. Whispering now she tried to calm the situation down.

"I was just worried when I woke up. Where's your ring, Michael?"

Stumbling to the kitchen island and without even looking back Michael muttered "I lost it" as if it didn't mean anything.

Putting her hand to her head whilst trying to control her shakes Sanne continued to reason with him.

"Ok, that's fine we are insured. I just wished you'd told me you were going out last night, I really wanted to talk to you."

"About what?" Michael snapped whilst trying to pour black coffee into a cup.

"It's Dad. He's staying on in Denmark, working on some case? I read it in the news"

Stopping suddenly, Michael turned to face Sanne. His face was almost pale with shock.

"What do you mean?"

"I don't know" whimpered Sanne, "Thomas told me and I've checked the local reports and it's true. A girl was murdered in the centre of the city."

Feeling his throat starting to tighten Michael threw his half filled cup of coffee at the sideboard and looked straight back towards Sanne.

Through gritted teeth, he shouted out "I'm so fucking fed up with your Dad, always digging, always sticking his nose in where it's not wanted, he was supposed to go to Denmark to get over your mum, not play the bloody hero again!"

Sanne's eyes widened as the tears now fell down her cheeks fast, "get over my mum? Sticking his nose in, "Michael how dare you!"

"No, how dare you!" shouted Michael as he started to head towards the door.

"How dare you and your pious family! You should all learn to stop looking down your noses at other people and sort yourselves out".

As Michael stormed out of the house and into the street he could feel his phone vibrating once more in his pocket. Realising that he had just run out of time, Michael knew he had to get away.

21

Odense, Denmark

They say that scenes in life can leave an imprint on the surroundings, and as soon as Simon arrived at Klosterhavn, although unaware of the tragedy which had taken place the night before, he seemed to have a slight unease about the place.

The leaves were blowing along the ground as if trying to sweep away the incredibly frenzied violence which had taken place on this very soil, and the birds tweeted loudly as though they were trying to convey their version of the horrors they had witnessed. It wasn't just an imprint: the wind was carrying the smell of death, and the magnificent cathedral that looked down upon the gardens cast a shadow that engulfed everything in darkness.

Simon had visited the Klosterhavn gardens many times with Vibeke; she had said that the locals neglected this beautiful garden, a small piece of wonder surrounded by chaos. The growing popularity of Denmark as a tourist attraction and the strong commitment of the Odense Tourism Board to turn the city centre into a large Hans Christian Andersen memorial had taken its toll on the locals' love of places such as Klosterhavn; and now it was hard to visit and not be bothered by confused tourists glancing at a map or large groups pushing their way through.

Simon walked through the parklands and was instantly greeted with news station vans. After Elsbet's high profile murder, it wasn't surprising that the local news had caught onto the biggest crime to happen in Odense in at least a decade. A reporter noticed Simon and pulled the cameraman along as she approached him, microphone heading straight for his face. Before Simon had the chance to react,

Jonas had jumped into the scene.

"We are not taking any questions at this time," Jonas said, pulling Simon away and under the yellow tape. The two men walked in silence towards the crime scene, and Simon noticed the blood on the concrete path. He didn't notice the body hanging above it until some time later. He took a step back and folded his arms.

"It has to be the same guy" Simon said to himself.

"Obviously" Jonas responded sarcastically. Simon ignored him.

"Well, look who decided to show up," Waage said, approaching the two men.

"I overslept." Simon said.

"Well lets put you to use. What stands out?" Waage said, folding his arms. Simon noticed the stranger next to him was giving him a similar look. Turning around to look at the body, he quickly closed his eyes and took a deep breath. A flash of Vibeke in their bed flickered in his mind, and he opened his eyes again. He looked up to the figure – an elderly man hanging on a large lamppost. Blood had trickled down from his neck and had formed a puddle underneath him. The man was high up – almost unnaturally high.

"This is similar to Elsbet's hanging, the hay in the mouth, hanging on a lamp post," Simon said, turning to Waage. He ignored Jonas, who was curiously watching in the background.

"Almost the same height, too What does that tell you?" Waage asked, and Simon felt as though he was being graded.

"It's the same killer. Someone abnormally tall"

"Who was that kid you held overnight?" Waage said, smirking again.

"Henrik, Elsbet's ex. He's tall" Jonas responded.

"But this obviously wasn't him" Simon said.

"Bengt, come over here," Waage said, ignoring Jonas. Bengt liked to take charge of a crime scene from the beginning and be the one to relay his findings personally, as he knew how easily the facts could be interpreted or embellished, and this was not something that he wanted to be associated with him and his work. As a graduate in forensic science from the University of Copenhagen many decades before, Bengt considered coming to a town he like this quite remote back when he was a twenty-eight-year-old with a Master's degree under his belt had made him feel superior to the country cops who came to him for information. Now an old man close to retirement, Bengt had a certain air of arrogance, and his unblemished career gave him the certainty that he actually deserved this right to lead from the front, and he figured everyone around him agreed.

Aside from being the only criminal technician stationed in Funen, Bengt also considered himself to be a highly respectable Christian, and would often question God why people did things that he was privy to all the time. The answer never came but Bengt trusted in God and understood free will. He felt his calling was to work with the victims, giving them as much dignity in the eyes of God as possible, a certain dignity they hadn't felt, down here, on Earth.

Bengt's wife Varda was his soulmate and, unbeknownst to him, she had watched him over the years when he'd shed a tear privately for certain victims. Varda knew that he sometimes struggled to reason with what was laid out before him, but in the end he always got to work, meticulously gathering as much evidence from the body as he could. She hoped that when retirement would finally arrive in a couple of years, Bengt would step down graciously and they would finally make the move permanently to Girona, Spain, where they had been enjoying their summers for thirty years to the point they had purchased a home there.

As Senior Criminal Technician from the National Police Forensic Centre, Bengt had been one of the first on the scene, alongside Waage. The two had always got along; perhaps it was their shared interest in theology and sociology that kept them busy on their weekends, often heading to each other's houses to share ideas. They always prided themselves on being the first and the best on the scene, and before Jonas had shown up this morning Waage had told Bengt to help him extra-carefully with the guidance, basically being told to spoon-feed Jonas where to go next.

"Bengt, how tall is our killer exactly?" Waage said.

"Almost seven foot. Easily. And he'd be strong, lifting the body up. We found bruises on the victim's arms that indicated he was lifted into position"

"Was he killed before he was hung?" Simon asked.

"He was alive when he was hung, but his throat had been cut. Nothing life threatening, more an attack to scare him. While there are some signs of a struggle with bruises, it seems he didn't put up much of a fight."

"Who is he? Is he a prominent figure like Elsbet?"

"Not at all. Erik Larsson, a retiree who volunteers to tend to the gardens here. His daughter has been calling us all morning. She's undoubtedly stressed. Erik was supposed to be at her house at half past five, but never showed up. She called him at around four-fifty and spoke to him. He was just locking up the garden by the church and he was going to take a bus."

"So he must've been killed shortly after the phone call. Why wasn't anyone around? It's not exactly late in the day" Simon said, looking around. For an early morning, the park was undoubtedly quiet: he saw a jogger by the river but besides that the park was empty.

"It is common here in Denmark, especially when the weather is like this" Waage said, motioning to the fog sitting over the park. Simon thought back to London and how a body like this wouldn't go unnoticed for more than five minutes. Only in the welfare state was it possible to consider a gruesome murder in the evening and have it go unnoticed.

"Well, we'll go pay a visit to the daughter. Get someone to run through security tapes, if any"

"Nothing. Go to the daughter's house, I'm going to appeal to the media. Two murders on public streets should have a witness. See if we can get anything that way." Waage said, indicating to Bengt to join him. The two men walked off and Simon turned to Jonas, who was standing behind the conversation with his hands in his pockets.

"Call the office. Get those kids released. From now on we do it my way" Simon said, and with that, he walked off to his car. Seeing the body had revived something in him. He was ready to fight.

22

London, United Kingdom

Sanne had wandered back upstairs to the children's bedroom and sat in the chair in the corner. Michael had bought the chair at an antique fair in Chelsea when Sanne first moved into his flat. It was for her to sit on in front of the dressing table mirror to tend to her make-up. It had been a kind gesture and was the first piece of slightly feminine furniture to enter the place. As time went by its needs and uses were altered. This was the chair which she had laid her weight on when she was heavily pregnant, both times; this was the chair where she had bonded with her children at night-time as she fed them, and this was the chair that she sat in to watch over them if ever they were poorly. But now it cradled her and gave her the comfort she needed. Sanne suddenly jumped up out of the chair when she heard the buzzer go. Fleeting down the stairs to answer it before it woke the children, she nearly tripped as she went. Expecting to see Michael but finding her brother on the doorstep, Sanne felt the tears start to stream and couldn't remember letting him in, falling to the floor and letting all the hurt and heartbreak that had built up over the last couple of months pour out. With Michael holding his sister as tightly as he could, they both stayed like that until his arms could no longer take her.

"Come on," said Thomas. "Let's sit up on the sofa."

Guiding his emotionally drained sister, Thomas led the way and was hoping amongst all hopes that she wasn't having a breakdown after the stress of their mother's death.

"Sanne, is it Mor?" asked Thomas, thinking he knew the answer. But he was shocked when she shook her head.

"It's Michael. I don't know what's going on with him. I was speaking to him this morning and he blew up completely."

"Did he hurt you?" interrupted Thomas.

"No. Not physically anyway. He stayed out all night and when I saw him this morning he got upset when I mentioned that Dad was helping out on that case in Denmark. He became so irratic and almost hit me."

Thomas could feel his anger start to rise. He knew it. Michael was finally starting to show his true colours. Selfish, money-grabbing and now a liar. Realising that he needed to take charge now that his mother was gone and his dad was in Denmark, Thomas went to get a tissue for Sanne to wipe her eyes. He grabbed some water for her and told her to go and have a wash before the children woke up.

"I will sort this, Sanne, don't worry. I am here for you and I won't let him hurt you or the children."

"Thank you," whispered Sanne as she took a sip from her water.

With that, Thomas headed off. He knew what he needed to do. What he should have done a long time ago. Head to the office and dig around Michael's paperwork and files. Michael was probably conducting the affair from work and that is where all the evidence would be. He would get this slimy bastard and make him pay for what he had done to his sister.

23

Odense, Denmark

Signe had spent the morning with a doctor after suffering a breakdown upon hearing the news. Simon and Jonas had waited patiently in a car outside her home, sitting almost in silence. Jonas too embarrassed to speak and Simon too annoyed they had wasted so much time chasing a dead end.

Signe had insisted that she should speak to the police, and the two detectives noticed her car pull into the driveway shortly after midday. They left their car in silence and followed her to her door. She saw them and motioned for the two men to come inside with her. Her eyes were swollen from the crying and she was still in her pyjamas, but Simon noticed she was a very Danish looking woman. He had been told in a brief call from the station that Signe was almost fifty years old, no children and had devoted a lot of her life to her business, which she had sold less than twelve months ago in a bid to slow down. Her pointed nose and pursed lips indicated that she had been a tough woman, and Simon could only imagine the conversation she had with the doctor in order to be released and come and speak to them.

Signe was composed when Jonas and Simon were ushered into the lounge where she was now stoically sitting. She seemed to be staring out of the window already, looking into the distance.

"He's not coming back." Simon whispered in his mind.

Jonas was the first to sit down in front of Signe, as her husband went off to get coffee.

This seemed to be quite a Danish tradition, Simon thought. Every house so far they had been to, under quite difficult scenarios, coffee seemed to be the medicine that idle parties went off to get. The smell of it was starting to leave an association of sadness in Simon's mind and he wondered if tea even existed in this country.

Fearing this would alienate him and was purely a selfish request on his part he agreed to coffee as well.

"Is it alright if we do this in English?" Simon said.

"Why? Aren't we in Denmark?" Signe pouted.

"You can speak Danish to me" Jonas added.

"I'm the detective in charge and I'd appreciate it" Simon added.

"Well, okay then. My English is not the best" Signe sighed.

Signe clasped her hands and didn't take her eyes away from the window, even when she started to speak.

"I always knew it, that something like this would happen".

"What do you mean?" enquired Simon as he took out his pad and searched for a pen, "Was your father frightened of someone?".

Simon offered Jonas his pen and Jonas said thank you.

For a moment, Signe moved her sight to the two men in front of her and continued in English whilst looking down at her hands.

"No, he didn't seem frightened of anyone that he mentioned, in fact quite the opposite, he was too relaxed with his safety".

Jonas smiled a knowing smile to show his acknowledgement of her fears. "This is normally such a safe place Signe, what happened to your father is incomprehensible, even for us".

Matt, the abiding husband, brought the coffee to the table and then perched next to his wife on the edge of the sofa, as if ready to jump up at any moment to bestow anyone of her requests. Simon knew how badly he wanted his wife to request something, just so he didn't have to sit and see her suffering.

"Erik was a man happy with his lot, Detective". stated Matt. "We keep going over who could have done this and why, but nothing is standing out to us".

Signe looked away from the window and directly at the two Detectives sitting in front of her. "I wish I'd told him how much I loved him" she whispered.

Uncomfortable by the emotions in the room Jonas turned to Simon indicating that he didn't know how to move forward with this conversation.

"I understand." Simon said, trying to stay composed.

As the walls felt like they were beginning to close in Matt suddenly stood up almost grateful for the interruption. "Erm detective," he said looking at Jonas "you have some coffee on your shirt," pointing to the stain which had formed on Jonas' stomach.

Embarrassed but a welcomed excuse, Jonas stood up and asked to use the sink in the kitchen.

For a second Simon thought he noticed a slight smile appear on Signe's lips.

"I think this is too soon Signe, we like to get as much information as possible as soon as possible after a crime but I don't think you can offer us anything else today.

Could we talk some more maybe later in the week."

Relieved at his suggestion Signe nodded in agreement and stood up gaining energy from her mistake in wanting to talk with them being recognised.

"We're leaving?" asked Jonas as he came back into the living room from the kitchen.

"Yes," said Simon taking hold of the situation "I've told Signe to phone us if she thinks of anything important, otherwise we will give her some time to get herself together and come back."

Smiling in agreement Jonas tried to discreetly hold his hand over the coffee stain on his shirt whilst awkwardly smiling.

As the two men started to head out of the door Simon noticed the photos of Erik placed neatly in a line along the dresser close to the door. Memories now he thought, nothing more nothing less.

"I'm a keen photographer," stated Signe, noticing what Simon was looking at.

As Jonas continued out of the door Simon suddenly stopped and picked up one of the photographs. "Where is this?"

"Oh, that was outside of my father's old school, where he used to work. We went back there last year as Dad wanted to see if it had changed. Nostalgic reasons I think. Why?"

"Nothing, I just recognised it." quipped Simon.

As Simon watched Signe close the door behind them he knew she would be straight back to the window waiting beyond all hope that she would see her father walking along their path again.

"Did you see that?" said Simon the second the men sat down in the car.

"What, the chaos? I think she's losing the plot, good call to come back later."

"No," said Simon "The photo of Erik. He worked at the same school as Elsbet."

"Coincidence" blurted out Jonas "Pure coincidence. Look Simon, the two deaths are in no way connected. The profiles are completely wrong. Different genders, different generations and different social circles. They couldn't be more different if they tried.

"But the killings are the same, the hay in the mouth" protested Simon. We had our killer, and you wanted him released!"

Starting the car Jonas smiled at Simon in a manner which could be seen as sarcastic.

"A copycat killer." surmised Jonas, "somehow he has found out how the girl's body was left. Maybe he saw it, her hanging there, got off on it as some people do and decided he needed to recreate that feeling. I think we learnt about this exact topic recently in one of these courses we are made to go on."

But Simon stared out of the window and for the first time, in this case, he was starting to think that it was bigger than them.

24

Odense, Denmark

Simon received the call from Bengt as soon as he got into the office. A note had been left on his desk to phone the pathologist back as soon as he could and after a couple of attempts and the line being engaged, Simon was eventually able to get hold of him.

"Sorry, we had a nasty car pile-up last night, two dead so I've been caught up, need to get home and grab some sleep so I can write up all the reports later on."

Simon was in awe of this man's dedication. For his age, he looked fit and healthy but moreover it was his attitude that impressed Simon. Dealing with death day in day out surely would start to grind most people down, but Bengt seemed to keep his voice at a level of joy on most occasions. Must be in his genes, Simon rationalised.

"No, it's fine Bengt, I've had other things to do too. Just wanted to return your call. Is it about Elsbet?"

"Yes, I thought you should know that preliminary findings alongside the obvious hanging are that she had ingested, over time, quite a large amount of Fluoxetine, Prozac, to the man on the street."

"Yes, I'm vaguely familiar with the name" Simon admitted without thinking how that sounded. He put Sanne's troubled past to the back of his mind.

"Is this unusual for you to find antidepressants in a young girl nowadays Bengt?"

"No, unfortunately not unusual, you are right, but it was the amount I found which puzzled me. These aren't easy drugs to get a hold off, either."

"Do you think she overdosed?" Simon asked.

"No, it's a lot but not enough for a suicide."

"Attempted suicide?"

"That is for you to find out. The hay found in Elsbet's mouth matched the hay found in Erik's. I've sent it off to conclude the type of hay and where exactly it comes from – not my speciality"

"So, they were killed by the same person?" Simon responded.

"Again, I'm not the detective."

"I'm asking for your professional opinion, Bengt"

"Right. Well yes, If I had to take an educated guess off the record, for now, I'd conclude they were killed by the same person." After, a civilised goodbye Simon put his to-do list to one side for the moment and decided that he would act now rather than later.

Just as he was weighing up the options, Jonas came in, with a certain bounce to his step.

"Let's go talk to Hektor and Helen, then. See how they knew Erik" Jonas said, taking a sip of his coffee. Simon motioned for Jonas to sit down, but he refused.

"Bengt called," Simon said, and before he had the chance to continue, Jonas cut him off.

"Let me guess – unrelated deaths?"

"The opposite. He believes they were killed by the same person. So that takes Hektor and Helen out of the equation. Something interesting, though, Elsbet had a large number of prescription drugs in her system"

"Suicide?" Jonas said strangely optimistically.

"Not enough to kill her, but close. It seems Elsbet was given a strong dose of antidepressants"

"So? Her ex-was back in town, could make anyone depressed."

"I think it goes beyond that. Her mother mentioned she had just started working at the boarding school, and now an ex-teacher from the same school ends up dead. I say we go and pay this school a visit. We also need to figure out who gave her these pills."

"Her father's her doctor, according to her files" Jonas responded.

"Well then let's stop by his place on the way. Tell the officers to let Hektor and Helen go, and offer your personal apology for insisting we lock them in prison overnight. From now on, I make the decisions" Simon scolded, and Jonas sunk into his chair like a boy into trouble. After listening to Jonas make the call, Simon motioned him to the car. Simon was taking this case back.

*

Martin made it clear from the start when he opened the door to Simon that this impromptu visit was an inconvenience to him. Simon had told Jonas to wait in the car, like a child, and had wanted to speak to Martin himself. Perhaps it was his own memories of Sanne's depression, but something about a father giving a daughter enough antidepressants to numb her angered Simon.

"I really have to head off in a minute detective. Can't this wait?" Martin said, putting on his trenchcoat.

"It's about Elsbet," Simon announced, in the hope, this may bring some interest out in the man.

"Maybe you can speak to my wife later detective, I'm sure she will be able to help you with any questions you have."

Incensed by the man's disregard of his daughter once more, Simon stepped forward blocking his exit to his laptop which he was just about to pick up.

"You want me to tell your wife you were feeding your daughter numerous prescription tablets?" Simon said, and Martin stopped in his tracks.

"Excuse me?"

"They have found a large quantity of Prozac in Elsbet's system which indicates it was taken over a short period of time but not enough to add towards a serious suicide attempt."

"Yes, I know how this works" Martin sighed.

"Was your daughter depressed? Suicidal?"

Simon added as he noted how evasive this man was and decided that he should just go for it now whilst he had his attention.

"That seems a bit out there, detective. Maybe I should speak to Waage about all this time you're wasting not finding her killer."

"The pathology reports don't lie. She had almost enough pills in her system to kill her," Simon continued, refusing to back down. "We can't just brush it under the carpet, so I suggest that if you know anything about this you tell me now before I have to start digging around further."

Seeing the man concede defeat in front of him Simon watched as Martin took a seat in the leather chair behind him. The chair had probably never been sat in, it was just for show, everything here seemed to be just for show.

"I gave them to her," Martin said with a now hoarse whisper.

"I'm aware of that; I want to know why."

"I prescribed them for her anxiety."

"Why was she anxious?"

"She was stressed. I didn't like how erratic she was becoming. She needed calming down and to get her focus back on what was important. She was going to ruin her career."

Simon stood closer now hovering over Martin who was staring ahead, avoiding Simon's eyes.

"How did you convince her to take Prozac, Sørensen."

"She trusts me, trusted me," he said trailing off and putting his head in his hands.

"I just told her I had something to calm her nerves, she agreed."

"Even if it put her in harm's way?" Simon said, and with that he left.

25

London, United Kingdom

Thomas was very wound up after leaving Sanne and the children. He could feel his anger starting to rise. Bastard. He had always known that Michael would do this. That Sanne would end up being hurt. To speak to her like that was disgusting but not surprising.

Thomas had suspected for a while that something was wrong with Michael.

It had kind of been dusted under the carpet since they had been trying to come to terms with his mum's death, and maybe that was how he had been able to get away with it for so long.

Thomas knew that any evidence on Michael would be at the office. It had to be: that was where Michael spent most of his time. Where in recent months he had slipped out continuously to make phone calls, where he organised his business trips up to their other branch in Manchester.

"Manchester!" Thomas shouted out as his walk quickly gained momentum and became a jog. Of course, there was no Manchester: probably some seedy hotel with his young whore instead.

Thomas was starting to feel a plan come into his mind of how he would get to the office and look through Michael's desk. If there had been business trips to Manchester he would have had to of filed for expenses with accounts. There should be a paper trail; if there wasn't, then Thomas had him.

Starting to feel slightly out of breath due to the adrenaline which was pumping around inside him rather than it being the twenty-minute jog he had just completed, Thomas breathlessly reached the office.

Despite not having his badge on him, Thomas knew it wouldn't be a problem.

It was the weekend and, although everything was locked up, Thomas knew the security guard to the entire building very well, and within a matter of moments of talking to him and saying how he needed some paperwork urgently, he was let in.

Making his way into the lift, Thomas pressed for the 12th floor. He took the time to stop and look at himself in the mirror.

A state of anger had taken over him, but why was he so pumped up that he might have caught his sister's husband in an affair? Shouldn't he feel sad for her that her marriage could be in jeopardy? Why instead did he feel a small sense of relief? Was he being selfish that he might finally be able to show Michael for what Thomas had always believed him to be? It felt strangely good.

Taking a deep breath as he exited the lift, Thomas headed down the corridor. Michael's desk was immaculate to the point of anal, Thomas thought. He was so up his own backside. Yes, Thomas' desk was a mess, but an organised mess and Thomas felt he gave more to people in the day rather than spending his time filing and shuffling paper.

He stopped for a moment as he realised the extent of his betrayal to his sister's husband and colleague, but then Thomas pictured Sanne's tear-stained face with his niece and nephew standing in the background, and he proceeded. Thomas would pick up the pieces.

After a couple of minutes, he was already becoming frustrated as he wasn't sure what he was expecting to find, but there was nothing untoward here.

No photos, no notes of a secret tryst meeting place, no receipt of champagne dinners. Nothing.

Starting to feel sweat appearing on his forehead, Thomas was frustrated with himself by the second as he came across account after account but nothing from Michael and Manchester for work or pleasure.

Sitting down in Michael's seat after another five minutes of searching, Thomas put his head in his hands. He wouldn't give up. There was a reason why Michael had been behaving the way he had these last few months, a reason why he had snapped so violently at Sanne and said the evil words he had, and a reason why he was now missing.

Michael was frustrated but knew he had another attempt on Monday when the offices opened again, and he could go to Accounts to see if there was any evidence that Michael had been to Manchester with someone else.

Standing up from the desk, Michael was about to walk away when a piece of paper caught his eye. He stood staring at it for a moment as his brain couldn't quite compute the word in this context.

It just said 'Vibeke' and around the name were lots of doodles, the type you do when half-heartedly listening on the phone.

Vibeke, Thomas said to himself. Why would Michael have his mum's name scribbled down on a piece of paper?

Turning the paper over, Thomas took a step back as he read the words.

"Bitch. Post letter. Phone DK."

Thomas went cold. Why was his mum's name on a piece of paper on Michael's desk? Why were these words written on the back, and what the hell did it all mean?

Screwing the paper up into a loose ball, Thomas shoved it into his coat pocket and headed back the way he came.

Staring ahead in thought, he nodded to the security guard who asked him if he had got what he needed. He said yes and then made his way out onto the streets.

The cold air slapped him in the face and a police siren in the distance brought him back out of his deep thoughts. Sanne, he had to get to Sanne.

Jumping into a taxi as his legs were now like jelly, Thomas realised what was upsetting him so much was the word 'Bitch'. How could his mum's name be anywhere near that word? What has this got to do with Michael's affair? Had Vibeke found out?

26

Odense, Denmark

Simon looked up at the imposing building in front of him and imagined it for a second through a child's eye. He was normally in awe of period architecture and for years had held a National Trust card back in the UK which had allowed Vibeke and himself to explore some of England's greatest listed buildings and manor houses

Although Vibeke had enjoyed their day trips out she often scoffed at having to pay to enter land in England because she was so used to the free roaming back in Denmark.

"England withholds so many beautiful secrets" she often said, "because it demands people to pay to see them".

She was right of course, Simon knew that but sometimes he liked to play Devil's advocate with her just so he could see the subtle pink shine in her cheeks when her temper rose ever so slightly.

Jonas rang the bell next to the weathered oak door whilst Simon noted how his Danish friend's confidence was starting to grow within their partnership.

"Well, you never told me what Martin said," Jonas said, irritated.

"All I know is Elsbet was stressed about something to do with this place" Simon muttered, looking around. After some time, a rather robust looking woman came to the door. She was wider than she was tall and had an eclectic collection of red frizzy hair protruding outwards, further emphasising her plump face.

"The door gets stuck quite a lot at the moment, I did try to buzz you in" she sighed as if it was their fault she was inconvenienced. Jonas took out his identity and showed it to the lady before she had any more time to offload her woes to them.

Slightly taken aback by the realisation that she had just been on the verge of being rude to the Police, the lady whose name badge said, Ida, stepped back and pointed them through to the reception area with her hands.

Being kept waiting Simon felt was a tactic used often to show dominance. They showed their cards so to speak and now it was the schools turn to pull back some control.

"How much longer?" asked Jonas without getting up from the leather chair Simon suspected he was wedged in.

"Not long I'm sure. The acting head is very busy but will be down as soon as he can."

"The police are busy too so if he is not down in the next ten minutes, we are going up." added Simon as he could start to feel himself getting frustrated with this charade.

Giving them a look of distaste yet again, the secretary buzzed for the third time on a machine in front of her and then pretended to look busy with some paperwork.

The acting heads reputation that he had built up with Jonas and Simon in the last 20 minutes did not proceed him. It must have taken him some guts to stand his ground and keep them waiting as he was nothing more than a slim rat looking type man who was holding on to the last threads of hair on his head making him look battered and ready for retirement. He introduced himself as Frederik Jessen and ushered them into a room just off from the reception area.

Not even up to his office smiled Simon to himself.

After the introductions and Jessen insisting that he didn't know how he could help them the three men sat for a few seconds in silence before the Danish-English duo began their repertoire.

"We haven't actually told you why we're here," pointed out Jonas, "So I'm not sure how you are so confident you can't help us."

Looking embarrassed for the first time the acting head acknowledged his faux-part and apologised, gesturing them to continue.

Feeling the ball was back in their court Simon took control now and laid out why they had come, stating that the school had come up a few times now in their enquiries.

Sensing that he was starting to become flustered in front of the detectives, Simon continued to push forward with his questions.

"How long have you been at the school?" he asked.

"Twelve years" replied Frederik.

"Twelve years" repeated Jonas in surprise. "That's an awful long time to be an acting head."

Frederik seemed to take offence to this but continued with what seemed suspiciously like a rehearsed answer.

"My father was friends with the old head and when the he left there was no one to take on the position. I had been working abroad at an international school when my father phoned me and asked me to step in, I guess just as a favour really to begin with but, well, here I am." he said gesturing to his body with his hands.

Simon moved forward in his seat and looked more intensely at the man, who was sweating on his brow.

Without having to say any more Frederik anticipated the next question.

"They kept me as acting because my orders still come from the retired head of school."

Breathing out as if he had just got a dirty secret off his chest the acting head seemed to sink back further into his chair. "In fact," he added, "I think I really should speak with him before I answer any more of your questions."

"We still have to talk to you," protested Jonas, and Simon stopped him from standing up.

"I need to make a phone call," Frederik said, and with that walked hastily towards the door and exited out into the reception area once more.

"I am going to have to ask you to leave," Frederik turned around without even stepping back inside the room. Ida came and stood next to him, Simon could only presume for moral support and for a second felt like they were probably a couple as they stood next to each other almost touching

"What!" Jonas said whilst standing up to face his evictors.

"You will need to get a warrant if you want to come into our school and ask questions." Ida said. Feeling Ida's and Frederik's eyes on them as they walked out through the corridor to the oak door Simon could feel Jonas next to him trying to control his anger. He knew that Jonas was having a bad day already, and figured shutting him down again wouldn't help the situation.

"I want to know who it was who put a stop to a few simple questions in there."

Simon stopped from getting into the car and looked at Jonas "It's not a question of who stopped us but why they did it"

As the two men drove back down the long driveway they lost sight of Frederik in the window of his office.

"They're leaving now," he said into the phone, eyeing the car as it left the grounds.

27

Odense, Denmark

The past makes itself known in strange ways. Simon recalled the dirty pub where he had met the young, blonde beauty that would one day become his wife, and in the last few months he had spent his time grieving over the fact that he would never see her beautiful face again. Now she only appeared in his dreams, and as her face faded from his memory he couldn't help but feel that maybe one day she would never be more than a dream. He dreamed and prayed that she would walk up to him and be with him again, and accepting that he would never see her had been a hard thought to bear. Assuming she had now become nothing more than the small collection of images he had of her, he never thought he'd see her again.

The corners of the diary pressed into his chest as he rode alongside Jonas towards the north of Odense and back to the cottage he had come to dread. He knew Jonas was talking but didn't pay attention to the words. He thought of the image he had found in the diary – the image of a fresh-faced blonde smiling and loving a life she would eventually voluntarily end. The thought that such a young and happy girl would end her life had him on the verge of tears, and he knew he had to keep looking forward so as not to alert Jonas that his grief had once again hit him.

Pulling up outside the cottage, Jonas parked the car and turned to Simon.

"Well, what did you make of that?" Jonas asked, visibly frustrated.

"They are clearly hiding something," Simon responded.

"Yes." Jonas answered, then after a long pause he sighed "Well, until tomorrow".

"Yes, see you tomorrow," Simon said briefly. He finally heard Jonas drive away as he approached the front door. Breathing a sigh of relief, he pressed his head against the door and felt its rough, wooden surface on his forehead. He knew he should look into the diary. Perhaps he was too afraid of seeing her again. He knew it contained all the answers he needed and he couldn't help but feel he needed to show Jonas. But he couldn't bring himself to open it up.

Turning around to the dark and abandoned road, he decided to walk a few blocks to the local pub. There he would find the comfort he was seeking. Alcohol was his greatest ally at the moment and he needed to forget everything from today.

The old pub that sat in the centre of the Odense suburb murmured with a familiarity of a small British pub in the middle of several small towns and serving no more than the locals. It had very little charm to it, and the dim lighting almost signalled that people not from here weren't welcome. Simon had remembered visiting the pub with Vibeke, but after her years of working in one similar to this, she was uninterested in eating the food and drinking the liquor. Simon tried not to think of the pub he met his wife in as he went inside.

Propping himself up on a bar with views out of the window, he ordered a bottle of red and sat back to enjoy the taste in privacy. The first glass went down with ease and he realised that forgetting his life wasn't going to be as hard as he thought. He looked out of the window at the dark streets and thought about anything else but the crime that he had been chasing all day. He wondered about the people in the homes across the street, the trees in their gardens, and then found himself reading the bottle out of desperation to forget.

"Does it say anything interesting?" a man next to him said in English. Simon was taken aback by an understandable greeting and figured the man had heard him order the bottle awkwardly to the Danish-speaking bartender. The man looked old and well-lived; his face was covered in wrinkles and his hunch showed many a year spent in front of a drink. His grey, thinning hair looked messy and his clothes unwashed. Simon didn't recognise the man, and at first, thought ignoring him was the best option. But he had read the bottle over three times and was looking for a new distraction.

"Unfortunately no. It's fairly standard," Simon responded, putting the bottle down and turning to shake his acquaintance's hand. The man shook obligingly and then rocked his beer bottle in his hands.

"You from around here?" he asked, taking a drink of his Tuborg.

"London," Simon responded, taking a sip of wine and feeling the bitterness of the red wash down his throat. He really hadn't grown to local wine here.

"What are you doing here, then?" the old man responded. Simon let out a forced laugh and looked down at his drink. He looked back down to his glass and realised he was terrible at making conversation and this man would grow tired of him eventually. He took another drink and motioned to the bartender to bring him a second bottle, throwing some kroner on the table for him to collect.

"My wife is from here" Simon blurted out, not entirely sure of what he was saying. The old man looked over to him and judged his appearance. Simon kept eye contact away and tried to hunch into himself as much as possible.

"And she let you out this late?" the old man responded, ordering a second Tuborg. Simon decided he could pay for his new friend's drink and pulled out some more kroner to throw away. The old man hinted at a smile in appreciation before opening the bottle and taking a long drink.

"She's dead, actually. Died a few months ago," Simon said. He could feel the old man watching him, but avoided his gaze.

"Oh, that's a shame. Death chases us all at some point. My wife died three years ago. Cancer," he said, taking another drink. Simon felt a strange feeling that he hadn't felt in some time. He found himself comforted by the man.

"I quite often go and sit by her grave and eat my lunch with her. I've planted a rose garden there and I while away the time talking to her." Shocked but not surprised at such a relaxed attitude to death, Simon wanted to dig deeper into this man's secret of coping with his loss.

"How do you live with it?" Simon asked, looking towards the man.

"Just how I can. In Denmark, we don't care for emotion. We don't express it because there is little need. I'm sure your wife spoke of the Law of Jante. We aren't above anyone. We aren't special. So who am I to exert my grief onto others?" the old man said. Simon had heard of this concept from Vibeke but always thought it to be rather silly and unnecessary.

"And you believe that?" Simon responded.

"It is in my nature to believe that, yes. And I've made it this far." The old man smiled. They finished their drinks in a comfortable silence and the old man stood up to leave. He nodded goodbye and left in silence. Simon sat there alone and deep in thought for another hour as he finished three glasses of wine. His thoughts jumped between his longing for Vibeke to walk through the pub door and the idea of Odense having a serial killer walking around. He thought of the victim's face, the hay, and the diary he had found with Vibeke's face. He pondered the idea of Vibeke being murdered before dismissing it as his own delusional thoughts. Perhaps he was not the right man for the case, and perhaps it had been a mistake to allow himself to willingly join a vital investigation.

The wine had hit him hard and he was feeling dizzy and close to vomiting. This was the first time he had spoken publicly about Vibeke and it had been to a stranger in a pub. The thoughts of his wife had depressed him, and he couldn't help but feel worried that in three years he'd be an old and ragged man drinking and considering himself unimportant. He could see himself becoming that now but knew it would kill Sanne if it remained. Feeling incredibly guilty about his selfish attitude, he hung his head as he walked home, trying instead to focus on remaining upright. Starting to rummage for his key in his pocket as the door came into view, Simon focused on getting inside.

The blow to the head from a blunt object came with such force that before he knew it he was lying incapacitated on the ground. The pain was instant, and confusion took over his mind. He was unsure as to what had happened and wondered if he had walked into the lamp which hung off of the wall to the side of the door. Slowly, as his vision came into focus, he noticed a man standing over him. His eyes were too blurry to make out the face, but he thought he heard Vibeke's name before the man left.

Falling back out of consciousness, Simon's mind was open and ready for it to be filled once more with his nightmares.

She stood there holding his hand. The leaves blew around their feet in a circular motion and Simon felt the temperature start to drop around him and them. Neither Vibeke or the boy looked at each other but they both looked directly ahead. The boy was almost grey in colour. His clothes were faded and his fingers looked skeletal like, clenched in between hers.
The silence was deafening between them and Simon could feel his heart start to race.
Vibeke had that look of concern on her face once more and had started to grey in colour. She seemed to have aged or maybe that

was just how Simon was seeing her now.

Within seconds the forest started to darken and a mist came down between the trees.

Feeling the tension, Simon was drawn to the boy once more. This time he could see that branches were starting to come out of the ground and grow up around his ankles. Not looking down the boy knew what was happening to him and opened his mouth, but screamed in silence.

The branches moved up his body, wrapping itself around him until they reached their clasped hands.

Picking their fingers apart, Simon could see that she was being slowly separated from the boy. The boy continued to scream in silence and Vibeke was now sobbing and shouting "No, leave us alone" on repeat, again and again.

The branches continued to cover the boy as Vibeke tried desperately in vain to pull them off of him. She moved quickly and continued to vent her anger as she went.

She screamed as the last branch tipped over his head and continued upwards until a tree now stood where the boy had been only moments before. Banging on the bark Simon felt like he didn't recognise her anger, her determination. She scratched at the bark until her hands started to bleed and she could continue no more.

28

Odense, Denmark

Jonas wife, Birgitte, quickly ended her call with Mads as soon as she heard Jonas come in; she had wandered into the kitchen to see how he was getting on but he was not there. She didn't know why she felt so guilty that Mads had just phoned her: it was just work they were discussing. She knew Mads liked her; that much was obvious and to some extent that excited her, but she wouldn't act upon it just yet. Divorces were ugly and if she had any chance of getting the next promotion she was in line for, she knew she couldn't afford to have any complications around her just now. After she got the promotion it would be a different story.

She loved Jonas to the point that she didn't want anything bad happening to him but that was as far as it went, and she questioned whether she was confusing feeling love for him with just feeling plain sorry for him. She had so many hopes for him when they first met. He was dedicated to his chosen career and she felt he had put his hillbilly farming days behind him. The courtship didn't last long before they moved in with each other and got married.

Birgitte was just starting out in her career and felt like they were both on the same track but the cracks began to appear, firstly when Jonas started to hint towards starting a family, which actually repulsed her, and then when she caught a glimpse of her husband in action as they socialised with other detectives and higher ranks. Jonas was the yes-man who always got a no. As a girl, she had imagined her and her husband having successful careers where they were the ones to give the commands, but as she grew older into middle age she realised she had married the type of man she always despised. In her younger years she had been too career-driven to find a potential husband, so when the time came where she was starting to see the signs of her age, she married the charming farm boy who seemed nice enough and respected her and her career. She had hoped that she could change his negative points.

He just didn't have it in him to move up and was so wet that he seemed to allow other people to climb all over him; as his career seemed to plateau, Birgitte's took off and the divide between them was starting to grow. Birgitte was surrounded at work by career-hungry men who gained power through sheer hard work but also manipulation and prowess, both qualities that Jonas had no clue. She had spent more and more time at the office away from Jonas in the week, and at weekends he spent time with his parents at the run-down shackle of a farm he stupidly felt guilty about leaving. This was fine by her and she enjoyed her freedom and had no intention of playing the role of Little Miss Wifey for Jonas in front of his boss, Waage, who, by all intentions, was the detective that Jonas could have been.

She had met Waage's wife Lotte a few times, and Lotte was the epitome of everything Birgitte would never be: the dull, dutiful wife who had no life outside of her husband's career. Birgitte had seen how Jonas looked at Lotte with a want in his eyes. But even that wasn't in a manly way; it was probably for Birgitte to be like her and nothing to do with a want for Lotte herself. She had always thought that Jonas would be better off with a boring and dim housewife like Lotte, though she never vocalised those opinions. Rather, she put on a happy face and did her best to make it through the social occasions.

Jonas had seemed distracted that morning and muttered something about the case. Birgitte had no interest in listening to her husband; years ago he had claimed that parking tickets were the big cases, while she sat by his side and watched Waage gain promotion after promotion, and newcomers like Romain overtake her husband in superiority. As usual, she was sure he had been set up to take the fall for the department and, again, as usual, he was so willing to be a lapdog that he had fallen for it hook, line and sinker. These days, she didn't ask about his work because she didn't want to know. And when she had asked, the sweat of his brows and stuttering of his speaking turned her off wanting to know more. He was still the loveable farm boy, and on those depressing nights, she questioned if she was the unlikeable one.

Birgitte finally found her husband and quickly went on to the defence for being kept so rudely waiting "I haven't cooked," she shouted in anticipation of Jonas asking, although admittedly that was his job more often than hers. "I presumed you would be home late again," she sighed whilst taking a sip from her white wine cooler.

Jonas entered the living room at this point and glanced at his wife who was now sprawled out on the sofa in front of the Jøtul, sipping from a ridiculously tall wine glass.

"I had to drop Simon home first," he muttered.

"Of course you did," retorted Birgitte as she turned the page of her magazine. Angered by her sarcasm, once more Jonas felt himself being pulled into her games and stopped himself from responding.

"I've got some paperwork to go over, I'll do it out in the kitchen so I can spread out" was all he could manage, and with that he took his bag and files pleased with himself that he hadn't risen to her bait this time.

Unwrapping the roll he had picked up from the café, Jonas started to spread all of the paperwork surrounding this case out in front of him and felt for the first time in a long time that he was actually doing the job he had signed up to do all those years ago.

Birgitte noticed that Jonas had eaten some sort of roll and was now drinking beer. He had obviously sorted himself out.

Jonas took a good few swigs of his beer before he had even sat down. He had seen sights that day that he had probably not seen for an extremely long time in his career. To see a man of a certain age thrown under a bush with his hand missing as if he was some piece of rubbish discarded, the thoughts immediately turned to his own father of a slightly older age and he noted that he would spend some time with him again this weekend, no matter how many snide remarks Birgitte made.

The beer was already starting to go to his head and he felt he had reached the Dutch courage stage he needed to return a call to Waage after his colleague had informed him by phone that Waage was trying to get hold of him.

"Waage," Jonas answered, clutching his beer in anticipation of the conversation that was to follow.

"Jonas – you didn't come back to the station today at all."

"Sorry, boss. Simon and I went to the school Elsbet and Erik worked at" Jonas said, taking a sip of beer.

"And?"

"They didn't let us in"

"Be in the office tomorrow, and make sure Simon's there" and with that Waage hung up. Jonas sighed and took another sip of his beer. He slumped into his chair and breathes a sigh of relief that the day was over.

29

Odense, Denmark

The morning came around too quickly as Simon woke, unsure as to how he had made it home from the pub, and could only vaguely remember a face that he spoke to the night before. Trying to prop himself up, the headache met him with force and pushed him back down onto the sofa. He had only had three bottles of wine, an amount he was becoming increasingly accustomed to, so he didn't understand where his headache was coming from. Lying there a little longer, Simon felt like he could very easily drift back off to sleep in the hope that his second awakening would be a smoother transition, but there was a feeling of unease which was starting to come over him and was preventing him from doing so. Then the thought of a man standing over him hit him. The man had mentioned Vibeke. He was unsure of the other words and struggled to convince himself it had actually happened. Struggling with his thoughts, Simon tried for the second time to prop himself up and this time succeeded, with the help of the sofa and some cushions. His head was throbbing even more now and his confusion was distracting him. Sitting alone trying to piece the evening together, Simon wasn't sure what he was remembering accurately and what his hung-over mind was fabricating.

Gingerly reaching for his phone, he had a message from Jonas saying that he was going to be there in half an hour, and another message from Sanne saying she was going to book him a flight home. This momentum was enough to increase the throbbing once more to the point that Simon slowly lowered himself back down.

After a few moments of weighing up both options whilst trying to recollect the night before, he came to a brief decision to tell Jonas he was heading home. Things were spiralling out of control here and Simon wasn't sure how much longer he could cope with everything that was going on. His headache was a reminder that he wasn't in control and maybe he just needed to head home before he did any serious damage. Feeling like he had made a decision through his confused state, he looked around the room trying to convince himself that he was comfortable with his choice and wasn't just running out on this place. As Simon's eyes strained to move around the room without igniting the throbbing once more, he suddenly caught sight of the diary that had been tossed aside. Recollecting that he had found Vibeke's face in Elsbet's journal, he instantly stopped in his thoughts and this time more successfully leveraged himself up to a more upright position. This seemed to propel his memory to work a bit harder and he was suddenly flooded with a flashback of the night before. Had he been attacked? That thought stayed with him a moment and as he tried hard to squeeze out more rational thoughts, he realised that he was starting to remember why his head throbbed more than usual.

Lifting himself to his feet, Simon winced as he moved over to the mirror above the Jøtul and took a look at the broken face looking back at him. Why had he been attacked? Steadying himself against the wall as a slight dizziness came over him, Simon shuffled back to the sofa for its protection. Here he questioned himself once more. Who had attacked him and what was their motive? He had an unease come over him again and realised he needed to stay on the case. He was obviously getting too close to something or someone.

Summoning his strength with new energy, Simon lifted himself slowly off the sofa and made his way tentatively into the kitchen to find some tablets. Drinking some fresh Danish tap water Simon felt a slightly clearer head starting to form but he still couldn't recollect his attacker's face, let alone the actual attack, in too much detail. Knowing that Jonas would, in fact, take longer than the anticipated journey time, Simon decided to head upstairs and shower.

Starting to realise that he understood his Danish counterparts' habitual ways, Simon was correct and indeed had enough time to shower and freshen up. With the throbbing starting to give way to nausea, Simon attempted to eat some toast before he heard a knocking at the door. Greeted by a look of disappointment from Jonas who quite clearly could see the effects of a heavy night's drinking, Simon decided to allow him these thoughts rather than blurt out his actual suspicions. He would keep this to himself for the time being. He sat in the car and the two men drove in silence.

The streets of Paddington that surrounded the police station seemed always to be in a constant flow of double-decker buses, taxis and tourists admiring the well-known London borough. Turning into a small Odense street, Simon hadn't assumed that this was where the Odense Police Station was, and when Jonas pulled into a small car park behind what looked like an apartment building, Simon wanted to ask why they had stopped somewhere along the way. However, when he noticed the singular police car and a small sign stating that this was the central station, Simon sighed and figured he should've assumed this much earlier.

Jonas guided him to a small interrogation room in the back corner of the tiny office, stating that his cubicle wasn't suitable because Waage would be able to find him. Simon knew Jonas didn't want him to see the dismal space a long-serving officer would receive, but figured it was best to keep that to himself.

While their attempts at keeping the boss away had succeeded, it seemed the lower-down staff members were able to point out the room furthest from the rest of the workplace and had interrupted

Simon and Jonas on three occasions. The first came from a long-nosed receptionist who appeared frail and permanently hunched in her stature, resembling that of a cartoon character, Simon thought to himself as he subconsciously rubbed the pain coming from his head which was already starting to work through the pain relief. She briefly let Jonas know that Avilda was at the main desk wanting to make a formal complaint about some youths she saw graffiti on a wall. Then came an Eastern European cleaner who spoke no Danish but was ushered out with various awkward hand signals and head shakes from Jonas. Lastly, two young cops were looking for a place to fill out some traffic report paperwork, and Jonas sternly reminded them that they, too, had their own cubicles.

The days of drinking too much were starting to catch up with Simon both mentally and physically, and after last night's attack Simon needed to try and clear his head as much as possible. So when Jonas announced that he was heading out to Cafe Hjem to collect some breakfast, Simon asked if June would be able to make him up a salad.

Before Simon remembered the horror Vibeke used to show when Simon would ask for food out of season, Jonas had made it clear with the look on his face that this was also an alien notion to him, and as he walked out of the station laughing, Simon was left standing in his own embarrassment, knowing that he would be getting a ham and cheese roll instead. Once Jonas made his return with a bag of pastries, they got to work sifting through papers. The morning had been a daze for Simon. He thought to the diary that he had rapidly tossed out of his coat pocket when he was getting ready for Jonas to pick him up. He thought of all the information it contained and how it would help a stumbling Jonas with the case.

But most of all he thought about how it had a young and fresh-faced image of Vibeke. The numbness that washed over his body was not only from the mild hangover he had woken up with after finishing the last of the four litres of the Beaujolais-Villages he had bought at the duty-free but also from the idea that he was so scared to see his wife again. Months of wishing for her and now he was turning away the one item he had to make himself feel close to her again. He thought back to the night in the bar where they met. He hadn't forgotten that night and thought about how soft her long, blonde hair had been when she first glanced over at him. It looked just like that in the photo.

Jonas bickered at the constant disturbances but soon settled back down at the table which, Simon noticed, gave him some difficulties when trying to tuck under with his slightly bulging stomach. Simon, wanting to guide Jonas in the right direction, thought back to what Anne had been telling him.

Much of the morning had been spent sifting through papers in silence. Neither of the men knew the direction to go in. Frustrated, Jonas threw his arms in the air and leant back.

*

The grey haired man entered the police station at a steady pace. He had spent the morning getting himself together as he felt that when entering official establishments like this, one must look their very best. He slowly made his way up the steps and pulled gently at the doors. After a minute of struggling, the receptionist came out from behind her desk area and helped him open the door from the inside. Taking his hat off of his head slightly to thank and greet her at the same time, Knuv, the old man, allowed her to help him into the reception area.

"How can I help you?" was the question that started the conversation off.

"I would like to speak with a Jonas Norgaard and the British man" requested Knuv.

"If you sit there, I will see if they are about. What is this in relation to?"

"I think I can help them with some information they are after." Realising that she wasn't going to get much more out of this old man, the receptionist made her way back to her desk and phoned through to the office that she knew the men were in. After a few minutes, the two detectives made their way down to the reception and instantly recognised from the receptionist's description, the old man that was waiting for them. Jonas stood back for a second and recollected that he, in fact, recognised this man from somewhere else.

"Have we met before?" Jonas asked as he took out his hand to shake the old man's.

"Do you go to the local church?" Knuv replied.

"No, sorry. Maybe I have just seen you around" replied Jonas.

"Norgaard, Norgaard very popular name," Knuv said.

"Yes, it is" Jonas responded half-heartedly, guiding the old man into the adjacent interview room.

"You wanted to speak with us?" interjected Simon, who by know was slightly frustrated with what seemed to be the usual greeting around here. Odense was small in relation to other places, yet people always seemed to be surprised that they vaguely recognised someone. But Simon felt almost hypocritical as he felt as though he knew this man himself.

"I did indeed," Knuv replied, trying to engage once more with Jonas.

"I've had a phone call from Frederik Jessen from Funens Dragskole and I thought I could be of some help to you. I was the Headmaster there for many years, until Frederik took over." Simon was suddenly more alert to this old man that was in front of them. At the moment, they would take any help they could get and for all this man knew he could be holding onto some important information without even realising it.

"What you like to begin, then." prompted Jonas.

"Yes, of course, you men must be very busy with all that is going on."

Smiling Simon sat back in his chair and assessed the old man in front of him. Every bit a headmaster through and through he thought. In fact, he reminded him of his when he was at school, Simon thought he looked firm but fair.

"Like I said, I had a phone call from Frederik Jessen. He thought maybe I could answer some of your questions."

"And what questions are those?" asked Simon, not surprised by Frederik's lack of courage.

"Well, nothing specific, just anything in relation to what you're working on."

"How did Frederik become the acting head?" asked Jonas.

"His father was a friend of mine. I decided that with my guidance he could put his teaching degree to good use."

"He seemed very offhand when we arrived," said Jonas as he passed some water to the old man whose voice was now starting to dry up.

"He said you still make decisions about the school. You would have been there when Erik Larsson worked there, did you have any say so in the employment of Elsbet Sørensen?"

"Elsbet. No, not really. Frederik ran it past me, I knew her and her parents from church so wasn't against her employment in any way. Such a tragedy." Knuv stated whilst lowering his head.

"What about Erik, then?" Simon reinforced.

"I had lots of teachers working under me during my time at Funen. I don't know them all personally" Knuv said, smiling.

"Well one of them was murdered, and we believe it's connected to a staff member you just said you helped hire. Surely there is something you can tell us about him"

"Well," Knuv said, acting like he was deep in thought, "Erik was a stern teacher, but fair. He dedicated his life to teaching and many students have him to thank for their education"

"Nothing suspicious about the fact they were both teachers from your school?" Simon asked, growing agitated.

"Funens Dragskole is the finest boarding school in Denmark. There is nothing connecting these crimes to the school. A media circus like this, well, it'll ruin the school's reputation. A reputation I worked to build." Simon watched as the old man stood up and put on his coat. "Look, gentlemen, I don't think the school has any relevance to this case if I can comment as a mere outsider. It's run like a tight ship and over the years we have had many inhabitants from Odense working for us." Simon raised his eyes slightly when he realised that this old man wasn't here with any relevant information but just to give his opinion.

"Thanks for coming in, Knuv," Jonas said, extending his arm for a handshake. Knuv obliged.

"Gentlemen I am happy to help in any way I can. I am at your disposable, so to speak and if I can be of any further assistance please come to me." Still giving off a self-importance that he had obviously acquired over the years of being in such a well-respected role, Jonas thought. He must be feeling quite out of it now. His school involved in an investigation and they had not gone to him. Jonas could sympathise with this man's feeling of redundancy.

"We will come to you if we have any more questions" Jonas reassured Knuv.

After helping the old man back out of the station and down the steps Jonas and Simon looked at each other.

"That was odd" Jonas smiled.

"A bit of a waste of time." stated Simon.

"Probably has Alzheimers or something similar," Jonas said, leaving the room.

"No, he seemed to know what he was doing" Simon said, but Jonas didn't hear him.

"What do you say about getting out of here?" Jonas said. Simon nodded and with that the two men headed for the exit. This caused Jonas to beam like a child, but Simon liked his eagerness. Just as Jonas and Simon were heading out of the station, the receptionist stopped them mid-flow and announced – indiscreetly so that the whole waiting area heard – that CPI Bøttger was waiting for them upstairs.

Feeling slightly caught in the headlights and sensing the eyes of the visitors on him, Jonas walked over to the desk and whispered back, as if to set a precedent for the following conversation from this young receptionist. Jonas told her that he was on his way to interview a victim and could she inform CPI Bøttger that he would go and see him when he got back? Not understanding the subtle hint, Trine responded at the same loud volume that a forensic officer by the name of Bengt was waiting for him in the waiting area and was here for the meeting as well. Turning around to view his visitor, who would have heard that his presence had just been announced, Jonas caught sight of him sitting in a chair slightly embarrassed by the situation and giving a wave of acknowledgement. Trine, after orchestrating unbeknownst to her a circus show for some of the visitors, huddled back to her post. Simon felt awkward for Jonas that yet again he had taken centre stage as a clown and tried quickly to ease the situation.

"Go ahead," Simon said. Bengt tapped Jonas on the back and Simon nodded before heading off. After collecting his surprise guest,

Jonas took Bengt up to Waage's office whilst making small talk on the way.

Waage had been waiting for his guests and had had his secretary supply them with coffee and buns. Just as he was on the phone with Lotte about possibly going out tonight for a meal, Waage heard the knocking at his door. By the weak knock, he presumed it was Jonas and congratulated himself in his head when that very person walked through the door. Bengt followed Jonas and shook hands with the CPI who had phoned him that morning requesting an urgent meeting about the cases which Bengt had been involved in these past weeks.

"Sit down please, gentlemen," gestured Waage. By the mere mention of 'gentlemen,' Jonas knew how this meeting was going to go. Waage's chest was puffed out and he was ready to play the in-control, sympathetic CPI in front of their guest. It was Jonas who first broke the uncomfortable silence as Waage poured the coffee, once again showing Bengt that he was a man of the people, one of the guys.

"Waage, Simon and I are heading out," Jonas said, trying to puff out his own chest.

"I see. Well, that is one of the reasons I asked you here. I'm concerned by our British friend. I have spoken with a contact in the Paddington Green Police Station and, although they wanted to remain anonymous, they were happy to relay back to me some information. Apparently, Simon Weller is unstable. His wife passed away and he didn't take it too well." Satisfied with what he thought was an obvious exploding statement, Waage leant back in his chair waiting for the reactions. Jonas turned to Bengt to firstly try to work out why this man had been brought into this obvious personal assassination meeting, and secondly to see if he would speak up to point out just that.

"I have to say I spoke with Detective Weller at the Larsson crime scene and he seemed very much in control of his thoughts and reactions. In fact, he offered some valuable theories," offered Bengt, blushing at the concept of betraying his friend's opinion. Jonas was pleased with his conclusion and watched as Waage's expression started to drop at the mere hint of disagreement with him.

Jonas took this opportunity to also defend Simon. "I have to disagree also, Waage, I'm afraid. Simon is bringing a new perspective to this investigation and his position here seems to be valid. I know he has suffered a loss but I think being away from where it all happened has given him some release." Feeling the insubordination starting to make his blood boil, Waage managed to calm it down internally and looked to Bengt directly.

"Waage, you don't want Copenhagen getting involved. We need someone and Simon seems to know what he's doing," Bengt added.

"Okay, I must take onboard what you have both said as you come from different perspectives on the case, but I would appreciate you both keeping a close eye on him. I fear he may be creating hype of a serial killer for the media," Waage smiled. Jonas opened his mouth to argue but felt Bengt nudge him on the side.

"Alright, fine. Now can I go?" Jonas asked. Waage nodded, avoiding any form of eye contact. Bengt follows Jonas in silence. As the two men walked back down the stairs in another silence they headed to the reception and fed a farewell. Bengt walked out of the station wondering what he had just witnessed. He was still confused as to why he had been included in on that meeting, but decided in his head that it was all for show, to put Jonas Nørgaard in his place in front of a spectator and undermine Simon, who seemed to be very much on the ball despite his grief.

30

Odense, Denmark

Pulling up along a small dirt track, Simon started to see the house appearing before him. It was most definitely a traditional Danish farmhouse, with its very low, triangular, orange-tiled roof, it was bricked at a slightly darker shade of brown and had windows dotted all around the façade in olive green. But you could tell money and style had been injected into it and Simon guessed this came from Jonas wife, Birgitte, and her very high-paying job at the city council. Jonas hadn't spoken at great length about his wife, and Simon wasn't sure if this was for his benefit so as not to upset his newfound British colleague who was in mourning for his wife, or if they just didn't have the same warm relationship that Simon and Vibeke had. Simon wasn't sure if he would get to meet Birgitte tonight to find out the answer, or if he would continue speculating. But, no matter what, Simon felt humble that Jonas, who appeared to be a very private man, was letting him have a small glimpse into his personal life.

The farmhouse was surrounded by fields and forest, and Simon daren't speculate how much of it Jonas owned.

"Why did you bring me here?" Simon asked groggily.

"You look like you need some downtime, and the office is no place for that"

"That's all well, but we are currently in the middle of an investigation"

"Yes, I know. I'll be honest with you, Waage is starting to doubt you. He spoke to your office back in London and, well, it's not good" Jonas said.

"What? What did they say?" Simon said, offended.

"They said you weren't fit to serve. Well, Waage is starting to believe them."

"And, let me guess, I'm fired?"

"Bengt and I supported you. But for Christ sakes, Simon, don't come into work hungover or smelling of alcohol." Jonas said. Simon nodded in embarrassment and looked around the property. Jonas read his mind and gave him an answer.

"It's not all ours, unfortunately. That's why I spend most weekends at my parents' farm, now that's a working farm. No sparkling new machines there or computers running the accounts, it's a good old-fashioned farm built up on blood, sweat, and tears. Birgitte says it's run-down but she doesn't understand: if a farm isn't grubby and used, then it's not a farm producing. This was our compromise, a farm building designed as a town house."

Simon saw the defeat in Jonas' eyes and guessed this wasn't the only thing he had had to compromise on in their marriage to make Birgitte happy. Simon decided he would go with the latter of his analyses from earlier and conclude that their marriage was not one of warmth or mutual respect. As they headed up to the front door, Simon noticed a work shed around the back of the house and smiled quietly to himself that Jonas did have a fire somewhere in his belly to retain some of his rights. He was sure that if he looked inside that workshop it would be pristine but muddled, used and grubby.

As they walked into the house, Simon could see what Jonas meant about it being a townhouse inside: the art on the walls would have been best suited in a gallery, and the very few bits of furniture had no use but were purely decorative. As they walked further into the kitchen, Simon could see that this very stylish, expensive kitchen with all the mod cons was very rarely used, and the table in the middle showed no signs of ever having occupants around it.

This could almost be a house where two people lived separately.

"I'm afraid we don't have a huge amount of food in the house, Simon, but I was thinking some bread, cheese, hams and soft drink would suffice, I have some crisps and things as well. Sorry, I was expecting Birgitte to be home and then maybe we could have made a bit more of an effort."

Simon smiled and pointed towards a wine cabinet sitting beside the bar. "Sorry, mate. I definitely prefer my wine," he said, doing his best to seem laid-back.

"Yes, I can smell it on you" Jonas responded, handed Simon a can of soft drink.

At that moment, Simon laid eyes on a note on the worktop which was signed Birgitte. He couldn't work out what it said but realised that Jonas hadn't read it properly either. He was obviously used to the fact that having a piece of paper on the worktop purely meant that Birgitte wouldn't be home, as simple as that.

In all honesty, Simon quite liked the change in beverage and cursed at the thought that he had given into someone's request; the first time since Vibeke had died.

Jonas did a good job of preparing the food and asked Simon to get the soft drink bottle for them fresh from the fridge, starting to get just a couple cans for himself. Simon noted how much Prosecco was in there and wondered how Jonas' farming parents viewed this city slicker who would be better suited in somewhere like New York, rather than farming territory out in the sticks of Odense.

They headed into the sitting room and this was as predictable as the rest, thought Simon whilst showing admiration of it to Jonas.

"You have a very nice home, Jonas. Our house here is a fraction of the size of yours." But the love and warmth it exudes are tenfold, he thought to himself.

At first, the evening started out on an introductory level of politeness, and Jonas gave Simon the low-down on the area and its inhabitants. Simon was relieved, as he didn't want anything too heavy, to begin with as he was actually enjoying the first decent food offering in a while. The beers seemed to go down too well as well, for both.

"Simon, I wonder if I can ask you why the London police have a reason to doubt you?" Jonas said this statement in quite a clinical way like a psychologist talking to a patient. The words lingered in the air for a moment, slicing through the friendly atmosphere that had just played out.

Both men were second-guessing each other's reactions. Jonas was half-expecting Simon to get up and walk out. But Simon had come to learn how the Danes approached subjects with clear, concise and almost clinical questions, and he took no offense at Jonas turning the conversation so abruptly.

Simon cleared his throat not only to stop any emotion that he felt rising at the mere mention of her name but also to pause for a second to work out what he was going to say. Because, if the truth be known, Simon didn't know where this was heading, if he was at all on the right track, or if he was doing any of this for the right reasons.

"My wife Vibeke killed herself a few months ago. It was completely out of the blue and if I'm honest I haven't coped at all with it," Simon said, stirring the glass out of desperation for a distraction.

"She was Danish?" Jonas said, cracking open another can.

"Yes, from Odense. I'm actually staying in the house she owned. I came here, I guess you could say in protest. Everything was miserable at home and I needed to get away. My daughter wanted to sell the house, and I…" Simon broke off. Jonas, feeling the situation was getting too emotional, handed his colleague another drink. This time it was a Carlsberg, something Simon hadn't had since he was in his twenties. Jonas gave him a soft smile and said "I won't tell anyone", and the two men clanked their cans together.

The Carlsberg had washed down well and taste had given Simon the best sleep he had had in months.

Simon recalled at some point in the early hours of the morning a woman who had entered the house and scoffed at the two men giggling in front of the television. Simon had attempted to work his charm on her, but it just caused her to purse her lips and announce she was going to bed and suggest they do the same.

The alarm sounded at 8:30 am, announcing to Simon that he had to get a move on with the day. At first, he didn't want to get out of bed and thought that waiting for Jonas to wake up felt much more relaxing, but the sharp pain returned as he remembered he had a key piece of evidence at home and he needed to get it for the case.

He was starting to like Jonas and wanted to help him. He didn't welcome this changing attitude nicely; he had wanted to hold onto his grief as much as possible. Maybe it was the Carlsberg and soft drink talking, but he had taken to this case and wanted to do his best to solve it.

Resolving that he needed to head home, he put on his clothes and attempted to sneak out of the door. Recalling that Sundays in Denmark were for rest and relaxation, he didn't want to wake up his hosts and attempted to keep as quiet as possible.

As he was approaching the front door, he was greeted by the woman from last night. The look of disgust on her face at his disheveled appearance was very apparent. He smiled and introduced himself.

"I'm just looking for Jonas," Simon lied, assuming that was better than saying he was sneaking out.

"I'm his wife. He's already left. I'll give you a ride home," she said.

"Where'd he go?" Simon asked, but he got no response. As he sat for the journey staring out of the window, he wondered how Jonas had put up with this woman for so long.

Getting out of the car, he courteously said thank you and noticed her judgmental looks at the cottage before he slammed the door and walked inside. He could feel her eyes burning into the back of him and he heard her put her foot on the accelerator and speed off.

Knowing that he should shower and make himself look presentable, he was overridden with desperation to view the diary and lunged for it as soon as he got inside.

Opening the pages, he felt as though he would understand Vibeke at last.

31

Odense, Denmark

Opening up the cafe at 6:00 am was a pleasure for June. Most people would struggle with the early starts and hefty delivery loads, but since the death of her beloved Angers, June had used the cafe as a means to face the day.

June and Angers had been married for thirty-three years and had had a wonderful relationship. They had met while studying science at the local university; both were born and bred in the land surrounding Odense and had used their love of the outdoors as a tool to guide them through life. The first signs that there were things wrong were the chest pains; even though he didn't let on at first, as the months passed he became thinner, paler and unable to move around. When he started to lose the feeling of his left arm, they went to the hospital. The news was bad – he needed a triple bypass urgently, but time wasn't on their side. God had other plans for him. Angers passed away three weeks before June's birthday. While at first, she had cursed him for his macho attitude of keeping it to himself, as a strong Christian she found her faith and eventually found comfort in seeing Angers at peace, no matter in what form.

Angers always had a strong, positive outlook on life and that had rubbed off on June. He had made her promise him that she would open the little café she had always dreamed of, a plan she had had since her teenage years and farm days. He told her how he would be looking down on her and would be with her no matter what. She was his heart and where she was, was home.

So 'Hjem fra Hjem' was born and June hadn't looked back.

October was coming to an end and the frost that had arrived at the beginning was slowly hardening: the soft white layer which gave everything a glistening shine was now starting to cause people problems. But June loved the months as they got colder. "Ice is God's way of mirroring nature so it can see its own beauty," Angers had said. "And when the snow comes, God's creatures know it's their time to rest."

As the delivery driver looked half-frozen to death, June hurried into the kitchen and made him a hot flask of coffee and a roll for him to take on the rest of his deliveries. She went into the kitchen to prepare so her staff could just come in and serve. Serving was God's work and she felt blessed to be able to feed this community with love through her food.

As June was putting the day's float into the till she was suddenly taken aback by a man standing in the doorway of the locked cafe. 6:00 am was normally a very quiet time in the town and the only people she usually saw were workers heading off to the train station or street cleaners doing a fine job of clearing up other people's laziness. June looked closer and realised the man was Jonas. Jonas didn't normally come until 7:30 am on the days when he was on early shift, or 5:00 pm when he was going home. Taking the key from her pocket she headed to the door and gestured to Jonas that she would unlock it.

Jonas stood there freezing cold with breath coming from his mouth. He had a hat on today, which June recollected was probably the first time this winter, and she could tell that he had maybe drunk a bit the night before.

"Come on in, Jonas, you will freeze out there."

"I was just going for an early walk before work and I saw the lights on. I hope I'm not disturbing you?"

June instinctively walked to the coffee machine to start it up as she reassured him that it was fine to come in. In fact, it gave her a reason to sit down for a moment to have a coffee herself.

"You look like you are carrying the weight of Odense on your shoulders, Jonas. I saw you on the news last night."

"Well, I feel like I am," he replied. Knowing exactly what Jonas was talking about, June brought the coffee to the table and poured it.

"I must say it is all very scary. You're leading the case with that British man

It's all very scary. Do you think he's targeting tourists? That girl was found near the Hans Christian Andersen house, wasn't she?" June looked scared and Jonas looked down at the table. He couldn't help but feel helpless – he didn't know how to comfort her.

"Jonas, what's wrong?" questioned June. "Are you worried about the case?"

"I'm worried I'm not up to it, June. I feel like I have to protect the whole of Odense and this is big. Bigger than me and I just don't know if I'm up to it anymore." Slouching his shoulders as if admitting defeat already, Jonas cut a sad figure in June's eyes. She had on a few rare occasions seen him out with his wife and had been sad at how she had heard him being spoken to. He had started frequenting the cafe more in recent months for a hot dinner when his wife was constantly at work, and here he was now trying to look after everyone in this town against a man who must have been extremely troubled, running around killing people. June wasn't sure of the words to comfort Jonas, so he just told him how she felt.

"Jonas, I am a lady living alone now due to my wonderful husband passing away. There are days when I feel quite alone, and as a woman of my age, that can be scary. But watching how you care so much about this town and its people warms my heart. You are alert and you care, and with those traits, you will be fine. Just keep on doing what you do and it will come good in the end. You mark my words. Good always rises over evil." With that, June stood up and went to get the cinnamon rolls which she had been heating up, and brought them back to the table.

"Now you eat this and get yourself together, ready for the day. Be confident, Jonas. You are a good man and you will work this out, I believe in you." As June sat down and took a sip of her coffee, Jonas felt his spirits start to rise. He was a good man and people did believe in him, he just needed to see it.

*

After another vision of a shadow in the corner, Simon was starting to grow weary from his mind playing tricks on him. Was it that or was someone following him?

He went back into the kitchen and poured himself a glass of milk, then decided to look through the diary. Sitting in the old semi-renovated cottage alone, Simon was surrounded by memories that he had spent so much time trying to forget. Over on the right facing wall of the living room were three different strokes of slightly differently coloured yellow paint. When Simon and Vibeke had first bought the house, Vibeke had stressed that before they do anything they had to paint one room.

Simon had argued against this, stating they needed to get the electrics and plumbing in order, and that could mean putting holes into walls if need be. Vibeke had wanted to create a sense of progress before the insides of the cottage were fixed, saying it would bring them positive energy if they saw the cottage was making some progress. In the end, she had gone to the hardware store on her own and brought back three test-size containers of paint. Simon had been out at the time, and when he returned she carried his hand into the living room to get his opinion on the choice. Simon had got angry with her, saying they weren't wasting money on paint when the walls may be torn down. It had made her upset, and consequently, the living room was the only room which was never painted. When Simon had seen it for the first time, he cursed himself for yelling at his wife for something so trivial. He wished she was here to finish the walls. He had drunk himself to sleep at the thought that he never apologised to her.

Sitting in the unfinished living room now, he felt a sense of calm. The feeling seemed both foreign and welcoming, and he felt his hands press against the small notebook that contained an image of a young Vibeke. She had long, blonde hair and a smile as wide as ever. She looked just like she had when they had met: young, happy, inspired. She was always creative and he loved that about her.

Simon sat in silence as he stared at the photo, his eyes meeting hers for the first time in months. Knowing that this may be the last new photo he might find of her, he wanted to savour the moment of seeing her for the first time. For the first time in a while, he felt happy.

Whilst looking at the image, the familiar cold sensation struck him, and before he knew it he was whisked away from his wife and placed in the real world. In his hands sat the crucial piece of evidence in solving the case. He had stolen this from the murdered girl who had been onto something.

Deciding he needed to show his partner, he reached for his mobile phone and dialed in Jonas' number. His finger hovered over the 'dial' button for some time and he considered whether or not this would actually work. Yes, he and Jonas were now getting along and he felt confident in working alongside the Dane on this case.

At the same time, Jonas was a Danish detective and Simon was no more than a foreign guest who had stolen evidence. Stolen. He repeated the word in his mind and immediately closed the phone. As much as he and Jonas were buddies, he knew stolen evidence would not sit well with Jonas and especially with Waage.

Looking back down at the diary, he noticed that there was another figure in the photo of Vibeke. Staring at the second face, Simon had a cold feeling that he'd seen him before. Tearing the photo in half, he put the photo of Vibeke down on the coffee table and the other half in his pocket.

32

Odense, Denmark

Everyone was so bloody incompetent. Birgitte felt like she was always picking up the pieces or glossing over their mistakes. As she ordered the new secretary out of her office to rewrite the whole draft letter, Birgitte could feel her temper about to explode.

These feelings of frustration brought her back to Jonas. What was going on with him right now? He had become so engrossed in this case that he was actually neglecting her. This made Birgitte even angrier at her secretary and she buzzed through to her, shortening the deadline by which the letter had to be finished. Feeling some relief from her emotions, she took her phone from her bag and reread the text Mads had sent her the night before. Jonas hadn't even inquired who the text was from when her phone had buzzed so late at night, too busy playing cops with that British man.

Now he was quite exciting to Birgitte's eyes. Rough-looking through some kind of personal demons, but quite obviously still in control of a lot of things. Jonas looked quite pathetic standing next to him, she thought, so why was she so disjointed by Jonas not paying her any attention?

She picked up her phone once more and this time tried to call Jonas only for it to go through to his answerphone.

Great, he was either out and about chasing around with his new best friend or filling his face at that June woman's cafe.

Birgitte pressed the buzzer to her secretary once more and demanded she enter her office again for another assignment: she would show this young girl that she at least was not losing her grip. Birgitte wandered along the road as fast as she could to her meeting in town; just as she was nearing her destination she caught sight of Jonas entering Cafe Hjem. "Bastard," she said out loud, as not more than a few minutes before when she had tried to reach him by his phone, he had told her he couldn't speak now as he was heading to a meeting, and yet here he was with his sidekick trailing into this eatery. As she headed on past, Birgitte could feel her heart pumping faster. How dare he treat her like this? The people at the meeting better not piss her off, because she was not in the mood.

Simon had received a call from Jonas to head to Café Hjem and had eagerly left the cottage. He knew he had to do something to lead Jonas along, and this was the best he could come up with. He shouldn't have torn up the photo, but he was left with few options. As he walked into the café, he received looks from the locals. The media hadn't let up about the British man assisting on the case and it seemed the whole town had been tuning into the investigation and the foreigner tracking him down. Jonas motioned to Simon to come and join him, and Simon did so almost obediently.

June attentively came over and in mediocre English told Jonas it was nice to see him again. Simon smiled inwardly at how suited these two people looked together, but dismissed the thought immediately. Once June had brought their coffees and a roll with ham and cheese to the table, she used her discretion and left the two detectives to it. Jonas pulled out the notebook and started flicking through the pages.

"Simon, our ass is on the line if we don't come up with something" Jonas said. Simon felt his body tense and needed to press on.

"I think we need to get answers from the school," Simon said. Jonas scribbled some notes down on his pad and took a bite of his roll.

"Well, it's the best lead we've got. Let's enjoy our breakfast and rest these hangovers," he said sternly, placing the pen down and focusing on the breakfast in front of him. Simon took a sip of his coffee and tried to find the best way to word what he needed to ask. Reaching into his coat pocket, he realised this was as good a time as any.

"I found this photo last night while cleaning the cottage. I'm trying to identify the boy" Simon said, passing the photo to Jonas. Jonas, reluctantly looking away from his breakfast, took the photo and studied it.

"Where did you find this?" he looked at Simon curiously.

He then called out something to June in a heavy dialectic, and when she came to look at the photo she let out a small gasp. Simon watched the two, desperate to pick up what they were seeing. June said something to Jonas and then looked to Simon before leaving.

"He's a well-known kid around here. It was a pretty secretive case. This boy hung himself on his family property. The property used to be one of the top businesses in Funen, but has died out completely," Jonas said, taking another sip of his coffee and passing the photo back to Simon.

"What is so secretive about it?" Simon said, studying the photo of the boy. He considered the eyes of the child, sensing a familiar gaze back at him.

"It's just odd. A boy dies in what looks like a suicide and the police cover it up as nothing more than a kid mucking about with farming tools. A lot of people didn't buy it, though whenever someone tries to reopen the case they get shut down immediately," Jonas said.

"You don't find that suspicious?" Simon asked.

"Well, when you put it that way…" Jonas started.

"Why do you think it's a suicide?" Simon asked. Jonas let out a soft smile and then called June over again, and they spoke together for some time. Then June turned to Simon and looked at him.

"He was a very smart kid. A prodigy. My mother knew his father.

His father would always say how this boy was going to make the farm a success. He wasn't a dumb boy, and he knew his way around a farm," June said, adding a smile to her sentences.

A voice from behind them piped up as it was heading out of the door.

"Yeah, some prodigy. Almost destroyed the school," Signe yelled, startling Simon and Jonas. June looked over to her in shock.

"Quiet, Signe. No yelling inside," June said, trying to make her otherwise squeaky voice sound dominant. Signe scoffed and left the café. It was apparent that the other customers trying to enjoy their Sunday coffee had overhead, and Simon and Jonas looked at each other knowing what they needed to do.

"What was that about?" Simon asked.

"Oh, several years ago someone tried to open the case, saying that the school he went to was involved. Gave the place a pretty nasty reputation: they've only just managed to gain it back," Jonas said, seemingly distracted by June serving customers.

"And what school was that?" Simon asked, already knowing the answer. Watching Jonas' face, he saw his eyes pop and his mouth drop.

"The very school we're investigating. Shit, Simon. There can't be a connection, surely," Jonas said. Simon knew there was. He could sense it. Everything was coming together.

"The school won't answer our questions," Simon said matter-of-factly.

"Shit, you're right" Jonas sighed.

"Didn't he have a brother?" June added, proud to be helping. Simon and Jonas looked at each other wide-eyed and then shuffled into their coats.

"Look, June. Thanks for the coffee." Jonas said. June smiled and dismissed herself and the two left the café.

On their way out, Jonas couldn't resist going over to the teenagers who had by now started to hassle passers-by with nothing more than laddish teenager behaviour: but for Jonas, this was not acceptable. He spoke to them and moved them on.

Jonas was going to clean up this town from top to bottom.

*

Signe was fuming as she exited the cafe. All the tittle-tattle that was going around recently was unbearable. Her father had been murdered and now they were trying to drag up old history which had been dead and buried a long time ago. Her father had suffered then: everyone had. The boy took his own life and that was tragic but it had nothing to do with anyone else. Yet the school had been brought into disrepute and that had weighed heavily on her father's mind. She would not have his name brought into all of this again.

Signe made her way to the bus stop and bought her ticket to Klosterhaven. She would go and sit there for a while as she had the day before. Although it was the place where her father had suffered his final moments, she felt close to him there and would talk to him about how she was feeling.

33

Odense, Denmark

Simon felt a sense of urgency as he sat in the passenger seat of Jonas' beat-up car. Whether or not the boy who killed himself had something to do with the various Odense killings had slipped his mind, and instead he felt himself focusing on what connection this child had to his wife. Jonas had ignorantly agreed that this was the correct path to be taking, but Simon knew once Waage found out he'd realise that it was a weak lead and that Jonas was indeed as incompetent as he thought.

Simon had taken a slight liking to Jonas recently, and he felt desperate because he wanted there to be a connection. He just had to find it. Simon had been known to act on impulse whilst on a case, and in the past this has got him into trouble. However, it also led him to things that others wouldn't even consider. Over the years he had learned not to question his actions, and that everything fell into place eventually, even if he had to make some wrong accusations first. God, please let this mean something, he thought to himself as the car approached the farm.

Instantly the old farmhouse looked like something Vibeke had always wanted to purchase and renovate. An old red cottage sat out the front, moss growing on the roof and a broken fence indicating the borders of the property. Large birch trees protected the property from outside eyes, and the brown grass was a stark contrast to neighbouring valleys of green. The cottage looked like it had once been loved, but in recent years had found itself neglected, as though the property had been abandoned. Maybe there was a newer and cleaner house out the back, Simon thought, but as they got closer he could see the train line behind the cottage and realised that this was it. Grief had hit this home, too.

Jonas parked the car outside the fence and they both got out simultaneously. They looked to each other in an attempt to locate the entrance to the property, and Jonas concluded that the best way to get in was to climb the fence. Simon thought to himself that a man of Jonas' age shouldn't be jumping fences, but he also remembered that Jonas was a farmer's son and in Denmark age didn't matter.

They approached the front door, and Jonas knocked on it sternly. It took some time for it to be answered, but slowly the front door opened. From within, it revealed a large man who Simon thought could be mistaken for a giant if such a thing existed. He was wearing dirty overalls, and his towering body looked like how Simon had felt after Vibeke had died. He looked like a true countryman, someone who had been excluded from society for so long. Simon felt uneasy being in front of him – while his grand stature seemed too foreign to be real, there was something unsettling about his face that almost felt familiar. Simon took a step back and realised that the face watched his with a similar horror.

Jonas spoke to the giant in Danish, and Simon picked up his name amongst the dialect-heavy tone in the officer's voice. Assuming this man didn't take too well to foreigners, Simon took another step back and left this interview in the hands of Jonas, who had seemed to forget that Simon was there.

The cottage gardens were long overgrown, and the front porch contained a large hole to the side of the front door. Simon also felt as though the building was leaning to one side, ready to collapse at the next gust of wind. He noticed some vehicles and made a mental note that the old Volvo had seen better days and they best check the registration number back at the station. The birch trees clouded the broken white picket fence, and the whole vibe of the farm felt as though it was not a farm at all but an old scrap shop with various odds and ends that nobody wanted anymore.

The sight of a particular pattern of garden on the edge of the fence caught Simon's eye. It wasn't unkempt like the rest of the garden and was even home to some small yellow flowers. A cracked tombstone sat amongst the flowers and Simon remembered the boy who ended his life. This must be his grave. He hoped that Jonas was asking about it.

Turning back to the giant, Simon noticed that he had kept his focus on what it was this foreigner was doing. Simon stared back at him, thinking of the photo he found in Elsbet's diary and how grief had brought these two men together. If only he could communicate what he was feeling about what this giant had gone through.

Hearing Jonas thank Jørn for his time, Simon felt as though he could only hint to the giant that he knew the situation and felt sorry for the man.

"Do you know Vibeke Lund?" Simon asked, feeling Jonas let out a small gasp beside him. The giant's face darkened and he took a step back. Simon thought for a second that it was shock, and the way his face sank into shadows made him think back to the night he had stumbled home and had been greeted by a blow to the head. The shadow felt similar, and Simon instantly felt like he wanted to leave.

The giant simply shook his head and Jonas thanked him and pushed Simon's back to indicate it was now time to leave. As they walked to the car, Simon felt his headache start to come back.

34

London, United Kingdom

He had to get out of here. Where could he go?

Michael frantically raced down the stairs of their flat and headed out into the cold, early morning air. A homeless person showed a sign in front of his face and it took all of Michael's strength not to attack this man. He probably has more money than me, Michael thought to himself as he hurried off into the London streets.

Not only was he still in debt, but also the people he owed money to were after him. He had been duped by the Danes who had promised help: not only had he not received a penny, but he was now also an accessory to murder.

It had all sounded so simple. Just a few letters and phone calls. He had been desperate. No one ever understood him. He was in danger of losing everything and he had to pay back the money. When the man had told him how Vibeke wanted to take Sanne and the children away, he had believed him. It had been harmless, just enough to scare her or at least make her apologise for whatever it was she had done. He had never meant for it to go that far.

Why did she kill herself, for God's sake? Why did she kill herself?

Michael shouted out a groan. He should have taken the other way out. End it all. But he knew deep down he had never been particularly brave, and if what this man was offering meant he could keep his life and get one over on the mother-in-law, it was a good situation.

But the money never materialised. The man wanted more and more from him, and Michael realised that he had signed his life over to the devil. The man was mad and when Michael suggested that he had sent enough letters and made enough phone calls, the man told Michael that he was in too deep. He would go to Vibeke himself and let her know just what her son-in-law had been up to.

The day Vibeke had killed herself was the start of a spiralling nightmare. Michael physically threw up when he was told. Sanne thought it was because of the shock but he knew what he had done. And then a few weeks ago he received a newspaper clipping from Denmark. There was no note; just the article. A young teacher had been killed. Michael knew they were connected.

That morning when Sanne showed him that her dad was on the case, he knew his time was up. No matter how bad Simon had grieved for her death, he was still a good detective and would eventually find Michael. He didn't know where he was going but he had to get away.

His life and his liberty were at stake.

Sanne and the children were gone. They were at the airport hotel waiting for the next morning flight to Denmark as a last-minute plan to save their father from his spiralling detective work, and Thomas knew this meant he could deal with Michael alone.

Thomas had tried to call his father, but of course this Danish serial killer was now taking all his time and Thomas couldn't help but feel at least his father was getting back to normal. He thought that his father being on this case was probably just a ruse to keep Sanne happy, and he would probably be caught out the moment Sanne and the children arrived at the cottage to the sight of his father in his favourite chair, drowning himself with his favourite beer. This would be the cross that his dad would have to bear. Thomas couldn't keep on picking up the pieces and trying to shake his father out of a depression. He had other things going on now and took full responsibility for his sister and her children.

Returning to Sanne's apartment, Thomas collapsed in a chair.

What was going on? What did the scribbles mean? Had Michael written them? Thomas stood up as the questions in his head brought on another burst of momentum and decided that he needed to dig further. He made his way to Michael's study, a room that Thomas always believed to be more for show than anything, and pulled at the door.

It was locked. Smart bastard, Thomas thought. With a burst of anger, he ran at the door and busted it open. The pain was instant and sharp but he felt like he deserved it. The study was dusty and typically pompous. It was everything that Thomas hated about Michael but he tried to focus. With the pain in his shoulder increasing, he switched to his other hand to start sifting through paperwork. When Thomas opened the bottom drawer he came across some phone bills.

Sitting down at the desk, Thomas opened up the folded paper and read down through the phone numbers in front of him. Nothing stood out to him at first. Numbers he would expect. Sanne phoning his mobile. Him phoning Sanne. Sanne phoning her parents. Michael phoning her parents. Thomas repeated this statement in his head for a second. Michael never phoned his parents.

35

Odense, Denmark

Driving back to Odense, Simon cradled his head and he tried to remember the exact figure that had confronted him after a drunken walk back to the cottage. He saw the faded, dark shadow in his mind and tried to focus on what the face had looked like. Had it been this Jørn?

The feeling of an intense stare from his partner caused him to lose his focus. Simon shuffled in his seat and searched for a way to reassure Jonas that he wasn't a grieving officer anymore.

"I'm sorry about what happened back there," Simon said as they reached the station.

"I told everyone you were fine. And then you go and blow an interview by bringing her up," Jonas said, his dialect shining through bouts of broken English. Simon wanted to tell Jonas why – the diary was sitting in his home and it contained the answers Jonas had lost sleep over.

"Well, what did Jørn say? Did he mention any teachers?" Simon said, trying to change the conversation. He watched the man contemplate what Simon had said and then released his grip from the steering wheel.

"He said that his brother killed himself as a kid: nothing new there. Jørn mentioned something about a girl who kept pressing him. The description matches Elsbet." Jonas said, turning onto the main highway into Odense. Simon felt the diary burning in his pocket. He had to confront Jonas.

"Elsbet was stressed about something. Perhaps she was researching the school and she spoke to Jørn about it" Simon said. At the mention of research, he felt the diary, which he had thrown into his pocket, burning into his sides. It was the one notebook in her bedroom, and possibly contained the answer to his questions.

"What about Erik, then?"

"Maybe Erik and Elsbet were working on the case together. Bring up the photographs of her bedroom"

As the two men sat back down, Jonas frantically started flipping through papers. He could smell the finale and needed to close this case. By the time they had reached the station Simon had made a pact with himself that he would offload slightly to Jonas and confess that he had taken Elsbet's diary, in the hope that one less burden on his mind might help him to sleep better at night.

Jonas was now cramming into his mouth the remnants of a pastry. He was such a secret eater, Simon thought. It was obvious to all every time Jonas took himself off to eat a sneaky snack, if only he didn't hide it. If he was that ashamed with his eating he should just cut back Simon rationalised but then smiled at his Danish friend's lack of willpower.

"Can't find his name here," Jonas said whilst trying hard to not chew down on the last mouthful as the pastry shards hanging out of his mouth were giving away his indiscretion.

"Tea?" asked Simon, alleviating the embarrassing stand-off.

"You don't have coffee?" Jonas asked childishly. Simon reached for the kettle and poured the black coffee into the mug. Agreeing that this would be his best shot at pacifying the situation before it had even started Simon took his time preparing to open the can of worms.

"Jonas, I have to tell you something. I want you to listen before you get angry."

Feeling below Jonas for the first time since he had started with the investigation in Denmark, Simon stopped what he was doing and just stared down at the cups which were now slightly over filled.

"I took Elsbet Sørensen's diary from her home."

"You did what?" Jonas shouted from behind him in a voice that Simon had not heard before.

"I needed to, Jonas. When I was looking through her room a photo of Vibeke fell out of a diary. I know it looks bad but I've treated it with respect, I just needed to see if I could get into the mind of Elsbet."

"Don't lie to me Simon. You did this for personal reasons, behind my back."

"The diary wasn't classified as evidence so technically I didn't tamper with evidence," said Simon now trying to justify to himself as well as Jonas.

"It's not about tampering with evidence it's about keeping it from me. We are supposed to rely on each other, you're so quick to pull other people up on honesty and doing the right thing and you've just completely done the exact opposite. I should report you for this. You've come over from England and now you show no regard for our procedures or my position. We could both get into trouble for this."

Simon was taken aback. He knew Jonas would be upset but not so angry.

"I just had to read it, to see if it gave us any clues into her death and Yes, I'll admit it, I wanted to see why Vibeke's photograph was in there."

"Then why didn't you bring it to my attention."

"I'm the detective on this case, remember that," Simon said, feeling his patience started to grow thin. Hearing his own words repeat back to him, Simon realised there was no going back from that statement.

"Oh really. By yourself. I'm not good enough, is that what you're saying to me."

"No, Jonas. You're sloppy, but you've been of use. So how about we stop yelling and you actually read through the bloody thing" Simon said, throwing the diary onto the table between the two men.

Jonas came out from the corner he had been standing in and came up closer to Simon. Looking up at the larger man in front of him Jonas started to speak but this time his voice was more controlled.

"The trust has gone Mr Weller. I'm not sure if I can cover your back so, for the time being, I suggest you concentrate on investigating this case through the proper channels and report to me everything you intend on doing."

"How about you stop pretending to play the innocent cop in all this and take a look at the diary. How about rather than worrying about your ego you help me find who killed these people" Simon growled. Jonas stood in the doorway and his head hung below his shoulders. Slouched over, he quietly closed the door and sat at the desk. Simon joined him and pushed the diary over to Jonas' side. Jonas, face pink from anger, picked it up and started looking through the pages.

"Your coffee," he said whilst pushing the cup out in front toward Jonas.

"I'm not thirsty. I have a bitter taste in my mouth." He grumbled. The two men then spent some time in silence; Jonas reading each page and Simon watching on. He would never admit it, but he needed Jonas. He certainly couldn't tell Jonas this, he wasn't even sure he'd have him as a friend after today. But looking at the man translate the diary, Simon was grateful he hadn't left.

36

Odense, Denmark

Three months earlier

It had been a long day and I was exhausted. I knew I was making the most of my degree, but day after day I felt as though my efforts were going unappreciated. It was easier when I was just starting out. Then everyone was interested in what I had to bring to the table. However, as I found myself digging further and further, I couldn't help but feel as though doors were closing and the friendly greetings had turned into cold glares and withdrawn pleasantries.

I sat over my laptop, letting the minute's meander past, and tried to put my thoughts into order. I sat back in my chair and listened to it creak. The office chair had been a gift from my father, bought at some upmarket seller in Copenhagen. He had told me that the leather was the finest, the wood the finest, and that I'd better make use of it. He had even bragged about the price, as though proud that a hefty price tag meant better quality furniture. It was all the same to me; I'd be just as happy with a 300 kroner chair from IKEA. I stretched out on it. The day at work had been so challenging. I felt the bed calling out from the other side of the room but knew my mind wasn't ready to let me rest.

I was getting used to this new routine. I was more than aware that I hadn't been myself recently: my blood pressure was too high, my throat was sore, and feelings of stress were overwhelming me. There was no such thing as a quiet day in my mind. I had always been this way, curious about the every day and the ordinary people that accompanied it. But something about this was different.

After work I had driven out to the property I felt was somehow connected to the building I put forty hours a week into. Sitting on the outskirts of Odense, I found it to be a long but pleasant drive on this long summers night. I wasn't worried about the darkness that would normally cast its spell on the rolling hills of Denmark; rather I was glad I was making this trip in the middle of summer when the sun barely set.

I remembered the feel of the rusted wooden gate on my hands as I had stood there struggling to push across the rustic lock. The man in question had been very insistent on locking up before I left, and I had gathered from the way he said it he didn't want any visitors ever again. I stood there for some time; observing the muddy ground while I questioned whether or not to make my way back. As I looked up to ask him just one more question, he was standing over me growling. He told me to leave and I knew right away it was an order rather than a statement.

It had taken me a week to build the confidence to come and speak with him. I knew he didn't want me digging, but I couldn't help but want to ask him more questions. I tossed and turned for seven nights about how to approach this man again. Lacking the courage to bang boastfully on his front door like I had the first time, I instead made the long drive to the property to leave a note in his postbox. I'll return again, and he can either greet me and welcome me inside or leave his rusty gate locked. He has two weeks before I make the journey again. Until then, I'll continue to dig.

Two months, two weeks earlier

Two weeks seemed to go on forever. I spent my days working quietly and waiting patiently. However, I wasn't fooling anyone and I began to grow agitated. I have exhausted my resources here and now feel the only way I can progress is through this man. Why do people have to be so complex?

He is one of the most puzzling men I've ever met. Most people I look into a predictable, as though they are following a formula. This makes it easy for me to decide whether or not I trust them, and I feel as though I've never been wrong in my judgment. This man, however, he was playing games with me. At least it felt like he was.

I have developed insomnia. I know how to diagnose myself, though my father didn't hesitate to lecture me on the symptoms I was showing as well as the outcome of the predicament I found myself in. He scolded me and tried to force me to take sleeping tablets, but I refused. I couldn't rest without knowing. My parents took their turns telling me why this was wrong, but in the end, they gave up and got on with their lives, and I got on with mine.

Today was the day. I went to work, as usual, smiled and exchanged feign pleasantries as usual, and at the end of the day, I got into my car as usual. However, instead of heading to my parent's house to listen to another lecture, I made the long journey out through the Danish countryside towards this man who had been causing me so much stress these last few weeks. I had debated with myself whether or not he would let me in, and not knowing the outcome was driving me crazy, I can admit that. I parked outside the fence and felt a huge sense of relief that the gate was now open. I felt myself at the realisation he was welcoming me in, though it did seem reluctant as the gate was only slightly open. But it was open enough for me to know what to do.

He didn't welcome me inside but instead gestured rather angrily. He led me through the house, which was run-down and very much unloved. He signalled to me to sit obligingly down to where he was pointing. The armchair was large and uncomfortable, dust floating above it and the spring digging into my bottom. I leaned forward to stop the dust gathering in my cardigan and watched as he pulled over a dining chair, dragging it along the rusted floorboards, and sat across from me.

The chair was just at the right eye level for me to see out through a small window, so I found myself observing my surroundings. The cracks in the window and the dust only highlighted the brokenness of the farm. I found myself struggling for breath not because of the dust gathering, but instead of the barn on the other side of the yard. It was *the barn*. Before I could take a proper look, I found the man watching me. The tension was growing in the room and I needed to ease it before I was removed from the house again. I tried some small talk, but it went unnoticed.

I moved to the reason I had come here. The work I had been building. He was hesitant to talk about the night or even the school I now teach at. For a moment I noticed he let his guard down as he started talking about the reason I had come here. His eyes opened just that slight bit wider, they looked to the left as if searching into the past, and at one point I think I saw a smile. Taking the moment I mentioned all the research I had done, as well as all the outcomes I found to this situation.

This changed his demeanor. He turned back into the coiled monster that had opened the door and greeted me. His fists clenched until the knuckles turned white, he started shouting vulgarities at me and as he did, foam appeared at his mouth and his face turned purple. He knocked the table next to him, which fell to its side, knocking over a vase that smashed upon impact.

"Get out" he had bellowed, "get out of our home and our lives. You sit in your big house and don't care about us. You just want some kind of excitement, to be a hero"

"No" I had protested as he pulled my arm, lifting me up from the armchair and towards the door. I felt my arm bruising and it began to go numb. I had tried to nudge out of his grip, but he is more than twice my size.

"Please, you have this all wrong. I want justice" I had cried. Spitting, the man stopped short of pushing me over the threshold.

"Justice" he repeated, "that will never happen, now leave us alone!" and as soon as my feet stepped onto the other side of the doorway, he slammed it in my face as if to put a full stop at the end of his sentence.

Shaking, I went back to my car. I sat in the driver's seat for some time and cried. I had been so close. I had seen the barn. I cursed my name and my parents and slammed my hands on the steering wheel. The arm he had held shot out in pain. As I left, I knew I was being watched.

Looking back at it now, I know I'm so close. I'm going to keep pushing on. I'll approach him again.

One month, one week earlier
I must admit I've taken my time in writing about this case. After the previous entry, I felt too shaken up to continue. I took some time off work and have only just removed the bandage that covered my arm. For the first week, I couldn't use the arm at all, and it became harder to hide that from my parents. My father brought home some antidepressants, which I must admit I've been taking. I've been having the longest dreams because of it. I dream of many things; mostly of my time in Sweden and of Henrik. But one dream stands out. It's of this stone-faced angel, telling me to keep digging.

I've been suffering a lot from sleep paralysis. I wake up in the middle of the night unable to move, and it's mostly during these horrific episodes that the angel appears. She looks so familiar and is so beautiful. I think she's the girl in the photograph I look at almost daily.

I'm feeling worse and worse and haven't heard anything.

I'm going to go to sleep now.

Three weeks earlier

I have woken from what felt like an eternal sleep and gone back to work, obviously on a cocktail of pills and painkillers. My arm seems to have a permanent bruise now, but luckily Denmark is never warm enough for me to remove my cardigan. I don't want to see that permanent reminder.

The school is imposing from every angle. Once you approach the driveway, it feels like it's sucking you in and you can't turn away. There is no hiding, no turning points, no secret arrivals. Everything is in plain sight, watching.

For as long as I can remember I've wanted to be a teacher, and after what felt like countless years gaining all the degrees required, I was so happy when I was given a job at what is considered Denmark's best and leading boarding school.

Some days I want to turn around and head back down the long driveway into the Danish countryside and back to that home, but I resist every day. I can't help but feel as though everything feels softer out there. The fields sway in the gentle wind, farmsteads are old and dilapidated but remind me of the old days. These softened lines gave off the appearance of kindness, in its own way.

My parents say I am too poetic for my own good, but I feel like that's what gets me through each day. I take my mind to a better place, especially when I feel uncomfortable. Perhaps that's the cocktail of drugs talking.

My parents are Denmark's elite. A surgeon and his beautiful, blonde wife. I was an only child, of course, they only wanted enough children to look like a family but not too many in which they'd actually have to take care of them. They didn't want to be distracted from their various social engagements. With that, I grew up with a nanny, but always felt pressured into maintaining my perfect appearance and equally perfect grades.

Today, though, my hair, which I get from my mother, is tied into a messy bun and my eyes, also from my ex-model mother, are hidden behind thick glasses. While I need the glasses for reading, I feel like they distract from the dark lines under my eyes. Yes, my insomnia had returned. I mentioned in my previous entry the angel. She began to grow more fearful, and the nightmare became intense. One night I woke to her gripping the same spot the man had gripped. I haven't been able to sleep since then, but at least she hasn't returned.

Today was different than the usual sluggish grind of the nine to five. As I pulled into my designated spot, I felt like I was being watched. Yes, I know what you're thinking. I always mention being watched, but there was something about today that made it stand out.

Standing at the entrance to the school, I felt something forcing me back. Almost telling not to go through. And part of me wanted to listen to that voice, but the other, more arrogant, part of me wanted to push on. I told myself no less than three times I can do this, and just as I was about to go in the school I felt someone behind me push.

Startled, I jumped back.

"Sorry" came the voice. It was one of the older year students, using the side entrance to get into the room. He must've been fed up with my standing in the doorway, but that wasn't a good enough excuse for scaring me.

"Should you be using this entrance?" I asked, adjusting my posture to what my mother had taught me.

Smirking, the boy gestured for me to enter through the doorway. "Yes, I'm helping set up the photography lab"

"Well, okay. If you have permission" I stumbled. The boy muttered something that sounded like an insult, but I let it go and made my way towards the library.

The library is the only place where I feel my nerves are at ease. I am a very big fan of history, as you know, and I love nothing more than reading the books this school has to offer. It reminds me of my days in University, though Henrik is not with me this time. He always seemed to know the stories I was eager to tell him, but that didn't annoy me. He was always interested in what I had to say, no matter how repetitive it was.

I sat down with a book on the history of Odense, eager to learn about the locals. I was reading for no more than five minutes when my phone began to buzz. Some students trying to cram in some early morning study glared at me as the noise echoed through the room, but I made sure to check the number carefully before picking it up.

"I told you not to call anymore" I whispered, assuming it was Henrik. He had been bothering me since we broke up, and while he had been quieter recently, I was sure it was him.

"History should stay in the past," the voice said. I didn't recognise the voice but recognised that he was trying to scare me.

"Who is this?" I asked reluctantly.

"You know who this is. Stop snooping, little girl" and with that the voice began to laugh. Almost a manic laugh. It reminded me of some of the dreams I was having. I hung up the phone and threw it into my bag.

The laugh has been following me all day, and I hope by writing it down now it will leave me. Everything is becoming so sinister.

Two weeks earlier
Everything is getting worse. Every felt like you've stepped into a

room and everyone has been talking about you? That has been every day at the school. Every day I walk between classrooms and feel as though a thousand eyes are watching me after just having spoken to me. Teachers are avoiding me, the students aren't listening to me, and last week I was almost involved in a car accident. I told my parents it was the driver who came out at me, but they are blaming my insomnia.

I haven't stopped digging, and at this point, I know I'm too far into it to just stop. It makes me cry almost daily as I know therefore everything is taking a turn for the worse, but I feel like I can't give in. I'm so stubborn.

Today was productive, though. The man, the one I visited months ago, he called me. I thought it was going to be the laughing man again, but I recognised the broken voice right away. He wants to meet me. He's willing to help me.

And at this point, I'm desperate for any help that comes my way.

The night of

I want to tell you about the boy that started all of this. I feel like this is the first day of the rest of my life. With his brother on my side, I'm going to find the truth once and for all. This is the happiest I've felt in such a long time. I'm so excited to finally be making some progress.

I must tell you about him. The whole story. Why now? I don't want this diary turning into a monologue of how terrible my life is. No, I want this to be a story of how I brought down the biggest boarding school in Denmark. How I uncovered their dirty little secrets and provided justice for the countless names of boys who have gone to that school.

What does the man have to do with it? He's the brother of one of the victims. The boy from the photograph with the angel. Tobias. When I was at his house the last time, before he threw me out and bruised me, he told me about Tobias. I never documented it as I was terrified, but it was the only time he's opened to me. I can tell you about it now. It would make an excellent introduction to this case. Here's what the farmer, the man I'm going to fight the school with, Jørn, told me:

Danish farming hadn't always been the glamour that was now portrayed in the media. The Ragelund farm had been built in the days before Denmark was a wealthy and progressive country. It had recently become an even smaller country, with Greenland being granted limited autonomy and forming their own parliament. Many had seen this as a sign of the times for their nation, and many didn't care too much. Vegard Eliksen was one such man who didn't care for politics. A Norwegian migrant, he had come to Denmark as a young man to seek his fortunes elsewhere. Where Denmark was suffering, Norway was suffering tenfold. Denmark was beginning to show signs of hope, and Vegard wanted to take this opportunity. Trained as a chef, he had found great inspiration through farming and, upon establishing his farm on the outskirts of Odense, he met with some restaurants and business owners and formed a strong relationship with the community. His combination of a love for nature and a love for food had turned his farm into one of the best businesses in Denmark. He was a smart man and always chose money over people. People were complex and business was not, in his opinion.

Vegard settled down in Denmark and found a wife who admired his dedication and at the same time kept well out of it. She became the devoted housewife, and her quietness and devotion made her perfect for the part.

Vegard's growing distaste at the world around him started when the Norwegians discovered oil. He felt as though he had been cursed for leaving a country that would strike rich, and it became one of the signs of his growing paranoia. He turned his wife into the punching bag, and while for many years he could keep his paranoia and anger hidden from clients, it was always on display at home.

On top of regularly beating his wife, Vegard had been pushing her to give him a son. He was now a middle-aged man and the farm work was becoming strenuous. He feared someone taking over the business, and after the constant refusals of bringing a child to their home, Vegard saw it best that his wife should be forced into becoming pregnant. After one attempt and nine months later, their first son was born. The boy was large for his size and had done serious damage to Vegard's wife, which wouldn't have bothered Vegard if not, for the fact, that he was beginning to realise that the son he had been blessed with was not in fact a blessing after all. The boy was oversized and slow. Vegard had given him the nickname 'Troll', as he both looked and acted like one.

When Troll was seven, Vegard decided it was time to have another son. The pain had caused his wife to die during childbirth, but Vegard was rewarded with another boy. Though this one was normal-sized, the damage had been too much and he had lost his wife. He immediately put Troll in the position of maintaining the house, and as the boy developed into a teenager he was only ever taught to clean and serve. As the elder son carried out this role, the younger son developed into a highly articulate and intelligent boy. Feeling as though everything was coming together, at last, Vegard praised his young son and began to teach him the farming business. By the time the boy was five years old, Vegard realised that his son was too intelligent to be out in the fields all day, and instead gave the elder son the job of maintaining the farm while the younger son would carry out the business, the mathematics, the money.

Vegard had been walking through the streets of Odense when he came across an advertisement for the top boarding school in Denmark: Funens Dragskole. Vegard rushed home and applied for a scholarship right away, and after three weeks and one interview the younger son had been awarded a scholarship and left for the boarding school, not to return until the summer. During this time, Vegard was left with Troll, and did his best to teach the boy to care for the farm. While his elder son would never be able to spell, or do simple maths, he was gifted at the tedious farm tasks, and Vegard was finally able to relax.

Despite being put at odds, the two boys admired each other greatly. At the start of the first summer, the elder son waited out on the picket fence that looked over the fields and waited for the bus to arrive with his younger brother on board. As he got off the bus, the elder son had noticed something was off. He looked malnourished: his bones were poking out and his hair was thin. His pale complexion was only made paler in the sunlight and his eyes looked tired. The elder boy was concerned as he approached him.

"Who did this?" he asked in his heavy dialect. The young boy looked down at the ground and shuffled his legs around. Feeling sorry for his brother, the elder son put his giant arms around the boy and cuddled him. Their family had never been one for conversation and they weren't going to try now. They walked to the cottage in silence, the elder son carrying the younger's bags.

That night at dinner their father had made a rare appearance from his study. He had begun to show signs of Alzheimer's, though he refused to go to the doctor and the elder son didn't know any better. He had also become paranoid towards anyone who approached the property and left it to the elder son to manage everything. This was beginning to have its effect on the business and the farm, with the property now appearing overgrown and ragged. The elder son didn't know any better and kept to his usual tasks. Now it was time to serve the food. He placed a bowl of stew on the table and served some to his father and brother. The father didn't eat it, he instead turned to a bottle of rum that had been left out the night before. He studied his younger son as he poured himself a glass.

"Are you still the top student?" the father asked. The boy nodded his head and avoided looking at his father.

"Are your grades the highest?" the father asked. The boy nodded his head again.

"Do your teachers recognise your talent?" The boy hesitated and then nodded reluctantly. The other brother could sense pain in the boy, though he didn't know what to do.

"Well hurry up and finish at the school; Troll here is running this place into the ground." the father laughed, slamming his glass down on the table and startling the two boys.

"But I must stay until I'm 18," the boy whimpered.

"Nonsense! You said you were the best. You'll be out of there in a year," the father said, pouring himself another glass. The rest of the meal was in silence, but the elder brother had a feeling that he needed to learn to take care of his little brother.

The long summer holiday had not been enough. Sure, the house smelled like pigs and their father remained locked in his study for the most part, but the boys felt a sense of safety and security being together. The younger boy had enjoyed being out in nature; he almost felt jealous that his elder brother got to spend every day outside tending to the animals. While everyone had said he was to grow up and be a mathematical genius, the boy had always secretly wanted to work outside. This morning was one of the last days of the summer holidays, and he had followed his big brother out into the fields at dawn. It was the middle of the season and he could sense his brother was glad to have someone there to help. His brother knew the land like the back of his hand – driving them kilometres out to a particular field that needed harvesting.

"What do you want me to do?" the younger brother said as they pulled up.

"Well, we need to clear the weeds. It involves driving this truck; I can do that and you can watch and see how it's done." The two brothers got into a large truck and the little brother spent the morning watching his brother at work. They ate in silence during lunch before getting back to work. A simple man, the younger brother had noticed how his elder brother kept to himself and didn't seem to have many friends. He was also incredibly large and strong, whereas the younger boy felt puny and weak.

He had enjoyed this day. And it was with that that he made the decision to confront his father on his schooling. He didn't like being sent away – the long school terms brought nothing but abuse and sadness for him. He wasn't passionate about sitting indoors and memorising formulas. He wanted to be out here in the country helping the family business and growing strong just like his brother.

They worked long into the night and returned when it was time for bed. When they returned, however, their father was sitting at the table, visibly drunk.

"I thought I told you to be home to make dinner," he said, pointing a finger at the elder son.

"I'm sorry, father. There was a lot of work today," the elder son responded.

"Did you get rid of the weeds?"

"Yes, but we need a new truck."

"Nonsense!" Vegard said, slamming down his glass. "The truck works fine. You aren't using it right." The room fell silent as the elder brother start to chop some potatoes and prepare a meal.

"I have to go back to school next Wednesday," the younger boy said, breaking the silence.

"Good, I need you to go there so you can come back and teach this idiot a thing or two," Vegard responded.

"I don't think I'll go back; I like working on the farm," the younger boy said.

The father looked him in the eyes for the first time since he returned home and glared intensely.

"You will go back to that school. That is how we will save this farm – you expect me to send Troll? That's funny," Vegard said.

"I don't like it there, Far. I don't fit in," the boy said. The father started laughing.

"That's life, son. You're getting on that bus whether you like it or not. End of discussion." The rest of the evening was in silence, and as they got ready to go to bed the elder son went to check on his brother and make sure he was comfortable.

"Are you okay?" he asked the boy, whose eyes were red and puffy.

"I can't go back there," he whimpered. The elder brother tried to comprehend what was being said, but all he could think of was how his brother was going to save him and the farm.

"If you go to school, you'll save me. The farm. The business. You can save us," the elder brother said. The younger brother stared at him and then shook his head.

"I'm sorry, I can't save you," he said. This made the elder brother angry and he left in a huff. He wanted to be saved and all he had heard was that his little brother would do this. He stormed into his bedroom and slammed the door. After punching his bedside table, he fell asleep for an hour before being awoken by an awful sinking feeling that he thought was guilt. Rushing to his little brother's room to apologise, he found the room empty. It was as though instinct had kicked in and he found himself heading to the barn. He didn't expect to find his little brother's body dangling from the room, but before he knew it he was cutting the body down and checking for signs of life. There were none and he cradled the body for the remainder of the night.

I have tears in my eyes writing this. I need to help this man and his brother, though passed. It's late, I should go.
    I'm going to meet the man who can help me put an end to all this.
    I'll write about how it went when I come home in a few hours.
    Until next time, diary.
    Elsbet Sørensen: crime fighter!

37

Odense, Denmark

"Well, this answers everything," Jonas said, throwing down the diary and folding his arms. He was going to continue reminding Simon of how he had destroyed the case, but there was a banging at the door.

"What are you doing here?" Jonas asked as he opened the door.

"I'm back from my leave. Who's this?" the man said. Enjar looked Simon up and down as the men crossed paths for the first time.

"This is Simon. Simon this is Enjar, Enjar this Simon." On cue, Simon his hand out to the man he had instantly taken a dislike to. His hand was met with nothing and for a second the two men stood rigid in their spots staring at each other.

"I've got the flu and wouldn't want you to get ill." said Ejnar.

Simon stayed where he was and keeping his eye contact with what he saw as a jumped-up idiot, put his hands out and signalled that it was fine.

Ejnar turned his attention back to Jonas who was looking awkward by the whole exchange.

"Well, I'll be seeing you soon, old man. Oh, by the way, Jonas, I'm enjoying the TV drama, although they do say the screen adds a few pounds to the body." Enjar laughed. Jonas, already agitated from Simon, closed the door in Ejnar's face and sat back down.

"Who is he talking about?" He sighed, clearly defeated. The tiny room in which Simon and Jonas had decided to carry out their research was small and smelled of mould. They had picked the room furthest from Waage's office, and for this, they had suffered a great deal in quality. However, with this room so isolated, they could carry on with the diary and the case that was unfolding rapidly before their eyes without Waage's prying. He had been too distracted all morning to even greet Jonas and Simon, and when they had received word that he had left they felt a sigh of relief.

"Well there was nothing about Erik in the clippings, but she circles a name multiple times. Knuv." Jonas said, pointing to several bits of paper.

"Wasn't he the old guy who came in to be interviewed?" Simon asked.

"Yes" Jonas said, smiling.

"Well, it was a strange interview," Simon said.

"He probably came in to make sure we weren't after him."

"Can we prove he's involved without the diary?"

"She has pages of newspapers about Knuv on her desk. She was stressed about the school, Jørn said she asked him questions about the school."

"And Erik?"

"He's an old teacher there, too. He could've been ready to speak out but Knuv killed him too. Come on, let's go" Jonas said, gathering his coat. Simon followed him as the two men left the room. Something about the case didn't feel right, but

Simon hadn't seen Jonas so excited about a case and was secretly interested in speaking to the headmaster. Something felt wrong about him and Simon needed to know what it was.

As they were leaving the station, Jonas noticed one of the young officers pacing uncomfortably on the other side of the door. He looked paler than how the winter made the Danes, and Jonas figured talking to another officer would take the stress of the case off his mind.

"You look like you've seen a ghost," Jonas said half-heartedly as he approached the young officer. A boy in his early twenties, the officer's blond hair poked out from the corners of his cap, and his bright blue eyes showed shock at Jonas' statement. Jonas thought that for such a young and cool-looking kid, he would be able to take the joke. However, it seems it had been lost and Jonas tried to rectify his statement, "It gets easier, working here."

"I don't think I'll ever get used to seeing dead bodies," the young officer spat out, almost angrily.

"What do you mean, dead bodies? What happened?" Jonas asked. He hadn't received word of another murder and he was the officer currently in charge of the biggest case. He figured his and Simon's office must've been well hidden.

"You didn't hear? Someone killed that old woman, Avilda," the officer remarked with his eyes wide. Jonas was shocked.

"What!?" shouted Jonas in pure disbelief. At his yell, the front door slammed shut and Simon approached Jonas. He didn't want to deal with the Brit now, and he pulled his car keys out and started heading towards his car. Simon followed him and pulled on Jonas' shoulder.

"Where do you think you're going? I just found something in the diary," Simon said as he tried to pull Jonas back, but it seemed that Jonas was stronger than he looked.

"Back off, Simon. Avilda has been murdered," Jonas said as he unlocked the car door. Simon could sense Jonas' anger and went over to the passenger side, getting in. Knuv would just have to wait for another hour.

38

Odense, Denmark

The drive up to Avilda's was one of silence. Simon could sense that Jonas was mulling over his last encounter with the lady whose body they were about to see. Death often brings guilt to those around it and plenty of 'what ifs' and 'if only'. Simon knew this all too well and felt a sense of sorrow for this Danish detective, who seemed to try so hard to 'do the right thing' but often got it wrong.

"We've all had them, you know," said Simon breaking the tension.

"Had what?" Jonas spat out as he squeezed the steering wheel.

"The local busybody, the town's nuisance who ended up just as vulnerable as the rest of us. You mustn't blame yourself."

"I don't. I just... just, I don't know, I just don't understand what is happening to this town." Sighing deeply as if to show he was mentally exhausted by it all, Jonas turned along what Simon presumed to be Avilda's driveway.

"This sounds like our killer is in a panic, by the way, the officer described the scene. Now that's worrying. Panic means more chaotic actions," Simon said. He wanted to keep Jonas on track, and secretly hoped this case was linked and would bring Jonas back onto the main case and therefore find Vibeke's killer.

Jonas could remember the last time he had been up here. It had been around seven weeks ago when Avilda made one of her frequent calls to the station. This time it was about a suspicious blue van, which she had supposedly seen come up her drive slowly and then turn around. He had convinced her that it would have been a wrong turning on the driver's part and that he would have had to keep going up to the house to have to turn around. Avilda scorned him for belittling her fears, but Jonas only felt frustration with the lady who called the police away from more pressing jobs every time she had a whim that someone wasn't doing what she expected of them. He had gone away cursing her name as he got back into his car. His day had started badly, he recollected, and he had carried that frustration around with him for most of the day. But had he got it dangerously wrong? Had that blue van which Avilda had been so scared of been up there to surveillance her home? Was she right that she would become a victim of a crime? Of course, it wasn't much long later that she did become involved in a crime when she across Elsbet's body and Jonas wondered if this had taken her thoughts away from the blue van.

Keeping his uncertainties to himself, Jonas got out of the car. The news stations had already arrived, and as soon as they noticed the detectives getting out of their car, they ran towards them, microphones in hand.

"Is this connected to Elsbet's death?" said the young reporter who seem too eager for being in such proximity to death. "Can you comment, Simon?" the reporters yelled as Simon and Jonas made their way towards the police tape and placed themselves comfortably on the other side.

"If this is our man again I'm wondering if Avilda saw more than she let on from that night," assessed Jonas.

"Or witnessed more than she knew she had" Simon added.

The detectives took a moment to take in the scene. The sky had almost frozen in its tracks. Any clouds that were in the sky was staying still. They were almost sheltering the darkness down below and the trees were doing the same from the sidelines.

This was the stark and eerie Danish countryside that Simon often witnessed for these few weeks of the year. It was in between the ending of the summer months and before the frost came out properly. Denmark felt destitute at this time of year Simon had always thought, or maybe he was just so used to London. There were some birds in the distance which seemed to be crying and the stillness was suddenly becoming overwhelming.

Walking forwards Simon took another side look at Jonas and could see how hard this was for him.

Bengt stood where the body was. The two men walked towards him slowly, trying to read his face as he began to meet their eye line.

"Anger, pure and simple," stated Bengt before they even had time to greet him.

"She was probably dead before she hit the ground. but the anger and psychosis seem to be similar. But I will hand that over to you. We are going to be here for some time as there are lots to do. I will leave this poor lady with some dignity of not having too many spectators and allow you to have a look, whilst I go and brief my team. But I should note that the hay wasn't stuffed in the mouth." He pulled down the white hood he was wearing, made an attempt at a smile, and walked off towards another tent that had been set up.

"Is it the same killer?" Simon asked.

"Doesn't look like it. She was stabbed, not hung." Bengt responded. Getting halfway he suddenly stopped and turned around whilst pulling down his face mask.

He shouted back to Jonas and Simon: "Looks like an agriculture sticking knife." he added, before making his way back to the tent.

Thanking him, the two officers proceeded over to their victim's body. Jonas was the first to move forward and lift the sheet that was covering what looked like a mound. Simon felt it only right that Jonas take that role.

"Dear God," said Jonas almost immediately, "Shit, what is our killer up to?"

For a second Simon saw him catch his breath. Keeping calm on the outside, Simon instantly had to control a reflux which was threatening to appear. He wasn't sure but he had a feeling that their killer was starting to panic, break down, and his irrational thoughts were taking over. This was the same guy. The statement, which Bengt had just relayed to them, was starting to register in his mind.

"How can this be connected to the case? Bengt said that the killer didn't put hay in Avilda's mouth. And her hands are still intact," Simon said to Jonas. Jonas thought about it for a second, but then something hit him and his face turned red.

"Knuv Clausen lives very close to here" Jonas stated. "I don't like how he keeps popping up close to our victims or the crime scenes. Maybe we should go and visit him now, he might well have seen something."

"Okay, let's go and speak to him," Simon added, with a sense of calm.

"I think at this point we need to pull any consistencies together."

39

London, United Kingdom

Thomas sat staring at the note all night. He hadn't slept, as it had circled around in his mind and invaded his dreams.

Rolling out of bed at what seemed to be becoming a regular early time, Thomas picked up the paper which he had left beside his bed and headed downstairs.

He had counted nearly sixty calls made to his parents' house and Mum's mobile in the last few months. Some calls to the mobile were at strange times of the night. Michael knew about the calls quite obviously, as he had the bills and they were in his name, so Thomas wondered whether Sanne did. What had Michael been calling Vibeke so relentlessly for and where had his anger for her come from?

Thomas took out his mobile whilst shaking and dialled Michael's mobile number. No answer. But Thomas didn't expect him one.

He then sent Michael a text:

I know what you've been up to with Mum. I have the evidence. Phone me or I am going to the police.

Thomas waited for about fifteen minutes and just as he was starting to wonder whether his bluff had worked, his phone rang from an unknown number.

"Thomas, it's me," said a very wary Michael on the other end.

"What the fuck have you done?" screamed Thomas.

He had wanted to stay composed and outwit Michael, but his emotions were getting the better of him and he knew his only way out was to bluff that he knew everything.

"Christ, Thomas, it wasn't my fault. I was desperate. They were going to do more than just break my legs if I didn't pay up. We would've lost everything. Sanne and the kids would have been out on the streets. It was the only way. I liked your mum, Thomas, I never thought she would do that. You must believe me. Can I talk to Sanne? I need to explain."

As a sick feeling started to wave Thomas over, he frantically tried to piece this information together as Michael was feeding it to him.

"I didn't know Mum would do it," kept playing out in his mind.

"But she did, didn't she? Because of you and all the phone calls," bluffed Thomas.

After a long pause, Thomas could sense Michael breaking down and unburdening to him. "I didn't know how vulnerable she was. I didn't know what had gone on. He just asked me to ruffle her feathers, that's all. God, Thomas, I'm so sorry. Please tell Sanne. I have lost everything."

Stumbling back, Thomas tried to reach out for the desk but missed and slumped in a heap on the floor.

"You bastard. Sanne knows as well and never wants to hear from you again. If you contact her or the children, I swear to God Dad and I will hunt you down." With that, Thomas terminated the call. He still didn't know exactly what it all meant, but he did know that Michael had been instrumental in his mum taking her life, and while it had sounded like Michael had been pressured into this, he figured this was nothing more than another lie. Fearing Sanne would also try and contact Michael, Thomas texted her under the pretense of asking if she was still waiting at the airport and how were the children.

Sanne replied almost immediately as if her phone was in her hand waiting for news.

"Still at airport. Waiting to board. Anything from Michael?" she texted.

Thomas tried to sound as matter-of-factly as he could when he replied "He called the home phone earlier. He has met someone else and won't be coming back. Mum had found out about it and was asking him to tell you. I'm so sorry, Sanne," Thomas lied. He knew this was going to upset her, but it was an easier story to take in than the truth.

Sanne's heart in that moment was ripped out. She had known deep down it would be something like that, but to read the words cut deep. She looked at Sam and Lucy and her heart broke again for their loss. If she could just get to Denmark, her dad would know what to do. She was lucky she had him and Thomas, they were the only family she had left now.

"Ok, I thought it was. Thank you, Thomas." The tears started to flow down Sanne's face as she watched the boarding lounge start to fill up.

*

Michael stood in Heathrow Terminal 3, looking for his flight on the departures screen. He never thought that it would end this way. Vibeke had always been so strong. He didn't understand why he had been chosen by the Danish man to carry this out or what even Vibeke had done, but he had been so desperate to get out of debt and get the loan sharks off his back that the money had been too good to refuse. He needed to get away now in case Sanne found out.

Waiting in the line for passport control, he agreed to himself that once he boarded the plane to Sydney there was no going back.

40

Odense, Denmark

The sleet had stopped for the time being, but Waage could feel the frost starting to freeze everything in place. Weather, especially in the wintertime, had a habit of tampering with their crime scenes. Furthermore, darkness was rapidly approaching which only made it harder to work. Waage had never found himself to be one for the cold; as a surfer, all his life he preferred beaches and sun and was already planning his trip down to Thailand so he could escape the Danish freeze.

After receiving the call from Bengt, he had told the secretary to cancel his afternoon and made his way to Avilda's via a restaurant where he had lunch with one of his university friends. He'd never had much to do with Avilda; he always considered her eccentric and nothing more than a paranoid old woman. Many in Odense knew of her and some, mainly from the church, seemed to care for her, but he never saw the appeal. She had tried to befriend him but had been turned off by his persona. He liked that, though. Although her murder had taken him aback slightly, he wasn't surprised, he had always wondered if her meddling would one day get her into trouble but this was something he could vocalise, and he if he was honest with himself he was only coming to the crime scene because Bengt had called on him.

He figured this was a good enough reason to take his time on the way.

Pulling up to where Waage could see the crime scene, he parked his car to the side then gestured to a young officer who was standing idly by and told him to move the car under some covering to the side of the property so it wouldn't be damaged. Waage pulled out to check his phone and was surprised to see that it was a call from Birgitte, a woman whom he had always questioned as to why she had settled for Jonas. She had never seemed like the kind of person to marry for love, but he still didn't understand her intentions. Sometimes she could put on an act that she had an interest in their work, and on the rare occasions when they would meet up for food she would always have a pained look on her face. His Lotte was a grounded lady. She was proud of her husband and he loved her for this. Waage had felt sorry for Jonas because of how he was treated by Birgitte, but this was always counterbalanced by Jonas' general attitude around the station. No, Jonas had run out of time. He had become a liability as far as Waage was concerned. Waage recollected his thoughts and saw Bengt approaching him.

"So what happened?" Waage said matter-of-factly. Bengt could instantly tell that Waage wasn't in the mood for mucking around.

"You mean Jonas didn't tell you? I told your secretary to pass on to you not to worry about coming out since Jonas and Simon have already been," Bengt said, showing obvious confusion. After all, they were almost packed up and ready to go, and Waage was almost three hours late.

"What do you mean, Jonas came here?" Waage said, fuming. He tried to maintain his composure in front of Bengt.

"I thought you had sent him. They left pretty quickly," Bengt said. Bengt was unflappable. That was how he had always conducted himself, but he was also no fool. Sensing Waage's mood, he dismissed himself and said he had to help his team finish packing up.

Standing there, Waage felt like he could explode, why hadn't they informed him that they were coming out here?

Offering his goodbyes to Bengt, Waage quickly gestured at a police officer to go and fetch his car for him and bring it back so he could head straight back to the station.

41

Billund, Denmark

The flight had gone without any dramas. Lucy, who didn't usually like flying, had settled down well by sleeping for most of the flight; Sanne was worried she was coming down with something as she was slightly hot, but now seemed to have caught her second wind and was running around inside the tiny car rental office at Billund Airport with her brother.

Sanne was nervous about driving in Denmark again. When she stopped and thought about it just before approaching the lady behind the desk, she realised that it was probably a good six years since she last had. Michael had always driven them before whenever they came out, and last year when she was here, it was her mum.

Filling in all the documents and securing the payment, Sanne felt very alone for the first time. Doing by herself what were normally joint actions. Was this how her father had been feeling the past few months?

Grabbing the children, she headed out to the car park and started searching for the car. The children found this a great game and their spirits were high yet again. Wondering if she had done the right thing, Sanne felt exhausted physically and mentally now and just wanted to fast-forward the next hour and twenty minutes and be at her parents' cottage.

She had not been able to get hold of her dad yet again and, although frustrating, she was convinced that he would probably have his phone switched off. He wasn't a huge fan of technology at the best of times and often let his phone's battery die out.

After a false start of stalling the car a few times on her way out of the car park, Sanne decided to head to the SuperBrugsen which was five minutes away and stock up on some food for the journey. She wasn't hungry and hadn't managed to eat properly since Michael had left, but she knew the children would be hungry and didn't want any upsets on the way whilst she concentrated on driving on the right.

She turned into the supermarket and parked on the end so as not to have to do any manoeuvres. The supermarket was a welcome place in a strange way: familiar sounds of Danish being spoken amongst families and smells of food which her mum always had in her kitchen in Denmark. Sometimes Sanne felt more Danish than English and coming back to Denmark always brought that home.

Lucy and Sam chose some items which probably weren't the best for travels, but Sanne was happy with any pacifiers for now.

Switching back into Danish with ease, Sanne thanked the kind-looking cashier who reminded her very much of her mum and headed back to the car.

As the chaos behind her ensued with the children arguing about who had what sweets, Sanne put her hands on the wheel and her head forward and took a deep breath in. Was this how it was going to be from now on? A solo parent, with all decisions landing on her. She would be mum, teacher and protector all in one.

The signs were there the last few months with Michael that something was wrong and so, although he had time to come to terms with what he was going to do, Sanne had not.

Starting up the car, Sanne headed to her parents' house to find comfort from her dad.

The children were asleep in the car when Sanne pulled up outside her parents' home.

That was fine with her because it gave her a few moments to take in seeing the house for the first time without her mum.

Sanne sat staring at a house which was a poignant reminder that her mum was gone. The garden was withering and the lights which normally illuminated handmade wooden structures that her mum had crafted, were in darkness.

She gripped the wheel of the car tighter and asked herself out loud, "What have you done, Sanne?"

She had just walked out on a chance of a reconciliation with her husband. Why?

Was she really that cold? Or was the fight just not worth fighting anymore?

Sanne was confused. She thought she had learned to love Michael.

Maybe the events of recent months had drained her more than she thought.

As Sam started to stir in the back, Sanne was shaken out of her emotional indulgence and turned around with a forced smile on her face to console her son.

"We're here, Sam," she whispered.

"Is Mor mor here?" questioned Sam whilst rubbing his eyes.

"In a way Sam, she is. Let's go and see if Grandad's home."

Lifting Lucy, who had now also woken, from the car, Sanne walked up the path and hoped her dad would be on the other side.

But the silence from the other side of the door told Sanne she would have to face entering the house by herself.

She found the emergency key hidden in its usual place and unlocked the front door.

It was the mustiness which hit her first. Not the smell but the actual presence of it. This house had always smelled of cinnamon bakes and coffee: it was as simple as that.

Seeing the worried looks on the children's faces, Sanne told them that Grandad had been too busy to tidy, but if they went and watched some TV she would try to tidy up a little bit and then cook something from what she could find in the cupboards.

Once the children were settled, Sanne went into the kitchen and rested her hands on the counter whilst she looked around the room. The state of the house had been a shock.

What had her dad been up to whilst he had been in Denmark, and where was he?

42

Odense, Denmark

Simon and Jonas pulled up outside Knuv's house and looked at each other before heading in.

They approached the front door and knocked. They were then greeted by the old man.

"Knuv Clausen" Simon said, as the old man slowly opened the door.

"Yes, hello Detectives again, can I help you?" Knuv said whilst still fragilely holding onto the end of the door.

"May we come in?" Simon said. The smile left the old man's face and he looked scared. He opened the door for Simon and Jonas.

"Please, my wife is sleeping," he said.

"We won't take long, but this is very urgent Hr Clausen."

Simon looked around at the house, it was as expected. Many books adorned the bookcases and shelves around the lounge. The television was small which signalled to the outside that a book took preference over the screen.

There were many certificates of excellence around the walls and a few old photos of the school and its pupils. But none of him and his wife, strange Simon thought but not unpredictable for such an academic.

"Gentlemen, please could we hurry this along, my wife isn't well and I'm sure she is getting nervous next door at our late-night visit from yourselves." Jonas requested Knuv should sit down and decided to go along the formal route of informing Knuv of Avilda's death.

"What, oh no, our dear, dear friend Avilda." stated Knuv whilst putting his head down in his hands.

"You were close then?" Simon questioned, "We weren't aware of this."

"We have been going to church with each other for many years, detective. My wife was particularly on good terms with her and for me, well, she was a familiarity around the town. We would often stop to talk and put the world to rights, that sort of thing."

"You haven't asked how she died," Jonas interjected as he could feel himself starting to becoming quite protective about this man's insincerity about his old adversary.

"Detectives that is not for me to pry. Now you said you wanted to ask me something."

"Did Avilda have any connection to the boarding school?" Simon quickly spat out

"Why ever would you ask that?" laughed Knuv as his eyes were starting to brighten up now.

Simon explained how the school was starting to link the crimes and this was the obvious route they were going to now investigate further. "You're barking up the wrong tree. That woman had nothing to do with my school."

"Don't tell us how to do our job Hr Clausen. We are going to magnify every possible connection until the killer or killers are caught."

"More than one killer? This is Odense. There can only be one killer here." Simon noted how Knuv had seemed to come alive, he no longer looked like a frail old man too weak to climb the steps or open the doors to their station.

Jonas moved over to Knuv's window and looked out at the view he might have had that evening, maybe he had seen someone heading up to Avilda's house.

"Do you recollect seeing a dark blue van around here over the past few weeks or anything else suspicious?"

"Well, now you come to mention it I think I did see a blue van, Jonas."

"Bollocks!" Simon shouted "He's playing games with us. You haven't seen any blue van have you."

Smiling Knuv leant forward and rested his head on the top of his walking stick.

"I kindly ask you to keep your voice down for my wife's sake. If you were one of my pupils I would be reprimanding you by now."

Simon could feel his hairs start to prick up as Knuv spoke, there seemed to be an element of enjoyment in his voice as he spoke now and Simon felt like it was time to take him out of his comfort zone and speak with him down at the station.

Requesting just that before they woke his wife Simon was surprised at how readily Knuv was prepared to come with them.

The phone call came through to Simon's phone just as they were guiding Knuv into the car. Simon wouldn't have normally answered it but the number came up private and that intrigued him.

Standing there as Jonas took over from him securing Knuv into the back Simon suddenly felt like his whole world had just come collapsing around him all over again.

"I'm going to kill Vibeke, you need to come home, just you, no one else." Then the caller hung up.

Trying to get his brain to take in what he had just heard Simon became confused, he could hear Jonas mumbling to him but wasn't making out what he was saying because the other words he had just heard kept playing repeatedly. Pressing redial Simon knew the caller would answer.

"Simon did you hear me, did you want me to drive," Jonas asked again for the third time

Grabbing the keys from Jonas' hand Simon ran first around to Knuv and pulled him from the car.

"We will speak to you later," he shouted to the old man who was clearly incensed at not being so important to them now.

And then around to the driver side as he shouted to Jonas to get in. "We're heading to mine." he shouted as he started the engine and shot forwards.

"Simon what's going on?"

"Just get Sanne up on speaker phone, now!" he shouted, "I need to see where she is!"

"You know where she is, London. Simon, what's going on?"

"I've got lots of missed calls from her on her Danish number, she's here Jonas and I think she's in trouble."

43

Odense, Denmark

Looking out from the kitchen, Sanne watched the trees blowing in the soft breeze. The call from her father had been panicked, and Sanne hadn't realised just what he had been up to. He had never brought work home with from him in London, at least as far as Sanne was aware of. Perhaps there had been times of danger that he had kept hidden from her, or maybe Denmark wasn't as safe as she believed.

Sanne walked over to the living room and pushed the curtain aside, looking out onto the street. She went from window to window, peered out and made sure they were firmly shut.

"Can I go to bed?" Lucy asked, rubbing her eyes for extra dramatic effect.

"No," Sanne said, "You have to stay here"

"Where's daddy?" she said.

"We can talk about that later. Now we are waiting for granddad to come home" she said, pushing the curtain shut.

"I wish Mor mor was here" Lucy whimpered, holding her bear tight and resting her head on it.

"Where's your brother?" Sanne asked, looking around the small cottage.

"Playing outside. Mormor put a swing there for us" Lucy said.

"Sam!" Sanne screamed, "sit here" she added, heading for the laundry.

"Wait"

She stopped.

"Don't leave me here" Lucy cried. She looked down to her daughter and then held out her hand. Lucy grasped it tightly.

"Don't let go, you hear me?" Sanne said. Lucy nodded and followed her mother outside. Walking towards the back door, Sanne hoped that her father would arrive home first. She listened for the sound of a car on the drive.

"Sam!" she screamed, noticing the boy on the swing set. His back was to her, and he was holding either side of the chain. Pushing himself slowly, he seemed deep in thought as he ignored his mother's cries. Before she had the chance to approach him, she heard something from the other side of the house. A tiny sound. At first, she assumed it came from outside. But then she was sure it came from behind her.

She knelt to Lucy and held back the tears of fear that were swelling in her eyes.

"Lucy, you listen to me. Take your brother and hide in the garden. Like you used to do with Mormor. We're playing hide and seek. Don't come out until I say so, understand?" She said, stroking her young daughter's shoulder.

"Is the bad man coming?" Lucy asked matter-of-factly.

"You do as I say. Take Sam and go now" Sanne responded. Lucy nodded and tip-toed out into the garden barefoot.

Sanne closed the laundry and turned around. She heard the sound again. It sounded like the hinge of a door, creaking in the wind. She went into the hallway and leant against the wall, waiting to peer in. She closed the door to the hall and glanced into the adjacent living room. Slowly walked over. Rested her head on the handle. Hesitated. Listened again for her father's car. Then she stepped into the living room. Immediately she wanted to scream. But instinctively she knew she mustn't, she had to be quiet.

Perfectly quiet.

*

"Fuck, fuck fuck!" Simon screamed and banged his fist onto the dashboard, making it quiver. "What's going on?"

The traffic had been ground to a halt on the main road into Odense. They had been waiting on the exit ramp for two minutes.

"It's the first snow of the season. Everyone slows down as most don't have their snow tyres on yet" Jonas said as though Simon was actually interested. Simon didn't answer but drummed his fingers on the dashboard. He weighed up the alternatives. There was a barricade of cars in front of and behind theirs, and all the sirens in the world couldn't get them to move. He could jump out and run, but he knew he'd be slower than the traffic.

It was quiet in the car. All he could hear was the humming of car engines and the patter of snow on the dashboard. The Volvo in front of them nudged forward a metre and Simon followed. Simon thought about who could've given him the call. He hadn't taken his eyes of Knuv the entire time, and it was impossible the call came from him. Then he knew why everything was starting to make sense, and he knew there wasn't a second to lose. Or – he tried to repress the thought – there was no need to hurry anymore. It was already too late.

*

As Lucy and Sam ran from the house they were confused by what was happening. The snow was falling harder and their mother hadn't given them time to put on their shoes and coats. This wasn't a normal game of hide and seek.

When Sam and Lucy had returned home from their last trip to

Dane-land, Sam had whined to Uncle Thomas about Mor mor's superior hide and seek skills and Uncle Thomas had told him about a secret spot in the garden that he would always hide in.

Mor mor wasn't here anymore and that made them sad. They had never seen so many of the adults around them cry before, but since Mor mor had gone that was all they saw.

Lucy was crying as she ran in her nightie. She clutched her brother's arm in one hand, and her bear in the other. The snow on her feet was cold and icy, and she wanted to go back indoors.

Guiding Lucy, Sam ran out to the hiding place in the garden where he knew if they waited long enough, Uncle Thomas would find them.

*

"He's in the house," Simon said. Jonas looked at him with incomprehension as Simon pressed the redial button on the phone. "I need to get Sanne out of there immediately. He said Vibeke was the last piece of the puzzle, but Vibeke isn't alive. He doesn't know that"

"Sanne is in the house?" Jonas asked.

"She arrived with the kids earlier. I told her not to come but she's so fucking stubborn. He said he was going to go to Vibeke, but he's only going to see Sanne. He doesn't know the difference; his mind is still stuck back to when his brother died. Fuck. Answer the phone, for Christ's sake!"

"Who is this 'he'?"

"It's Jørn. It all makes sense now. He's been going after those he believe had something to do with his brother's suicide. Elsbet was investigating, Erik was his old teacher and Knuv was the headmaster" Simon said.

"What does your wife have to do with it, then?" Jonas said. Simon nudged further forward in the traffic.

"Remember that photo I showed you of the boy? I ripped it in half. It was a photo of Vibeke and the boy. I don't know how she knew him but she did." Simon said.

"But Avilda has no relation to the school," Jonas said, growing frustrated.

"We'll find a connection later. Fuck, why isn't she answering the phone?"

"We'll send another police car," Jonas said, reaching for his phone.

"No!" Simon snapped. "It's too late anyway. He's got them. And the only chance we have now is me."

"You?"

"Yes. He told me I had to come. If someone else shows up he'll kill them"

"You're not part of this, Simon. It makes no sense"

"No. I am a part. He's waiting for me" Jonas shot a glance to Simon as he heard the engine ahead of them nudge forward further.

"You think he is?"

"Yes," Simon said, catching sight of the car in the wing mirror.

*

Sanne struggled to break free but went limp in the man's iron grip when she felt the cold steel on his throat.

"This knife has been in my family for over sixty years. Used to use it to kill pigs. You wouldn't believe how easy it is"

The man told her to open wide, and shoved what felt and smelled like hay into her mouth. He ordered her to lie on her stomach with her arms behind her back.

As Sanne didn't obey at once the knife was thrust in under her ear and she felt hot blood coursing over her shoulder and inside her t-shirt. She lay on her stomach on the floorboards and the man sat on top of her, his weight crushing her body into the floor. She felt the plastic of ties cut into the skin around her wrists. She was then lifted and dropped onto the sofa. Before she had the chance to kick, he tied her ankles together and forced her back into the sofa.

She watched as the man started pushing all the furniture to the side, leaving space underneath a chandelier her mother had fastened during the renovations. He pushed it so carelessly that one of the tables broke, and Sanne tried to scream at him.

"He was innocent boy. Intelligent, kind. He was going to save our family" the man said, throwing cushions off a chair. Sanne tried to lift herself off the sofa but before she had the chance he had wrapped his arm around her.

"Why didn't you help him?" he said, wrapping a rope around her neck and fastening. Sanne felt the fibres push into her throat and struggled to find breath.

"Now you'll die. Just like he did"

*

The car sped along the suburban streets of outer Odense. Simon accelerated up the drive towards the odd-looking wooden house he and Vibeke had called home, but in the sharp turn as he pulled in the wheels spun on the fresh snow and he felt the car losing its grip. He didn't try to correct it, but let the car crash into the tree that sat out the front of the property. Before he and Jonas had time to make sure one another were okay, Simon was already running towards the cottage.

He couldn't see any footprints in the snow leading up to the house as he continued to bound up towards the door.

He went towards the sound that was coming from the living room. He could feel it now, as pressure on his temples, this was where it would end. And there was logic to it. How many times had he talked about the potential this room had with Vibeke, day after day, only to have her gone before she could see the end to it. He had travelled all this way desperate to feel some connection to her, but he hadn't found it. The nightmares had followed him here and there was no escaping it now.

Reaching for the toolbox that sat in the front entrance, he pulled out a hammer and a box cutting knife. He felt the cold of the metal against his fingertips as he placed it into his coat pocket.

He turned into the living room and saw her there. Sanne's eyes were wide and black. Her head strained towards the ceiling as though she was trying to see over a fence, and from this position she stared back down and looked at him. Her shoulders were pulled back and her arms were hidden, and Simon assumed that her hands had been tied. She was standing on one of the dining room chairs that Vibeke had chosen from a flea market. A red wooden chair that didn't match any of the other ones that sat around the dining table. Sanne was standing on her toes and struggling to maintain her balance. Her cheeks bulged as though she had a sock or a cloth in her mouth. Her neck was wrapped in a rope that was connected to the chandelier in the middle of the living room. She was so close to falling.

Sanne was staring back at her father without blinking. The muscles in her face were twitching, alternating between fury and naked fear.

Jonas had crept up behind Simon and was now standing behind her. She gave her father a desperate look, asking him to come and save her. Simon understood.

"Well?" Jonas whispered, his eyes fixated on Sanne.

"He's left. Keep an eye on the door" Simon said, running for his daughter. Looking up at her, he pulled a spare chair over to her and stood on it. He cut the rope from the chandelier and felt his daughter collapse into his arms. He cut the tie from her wrists and jumped down to cut it from her ankles. She fell to the floor, sobbing.

"The kids" she cried, wrapping her arms around her father.

"We'll find them. Are you okay?" Simon said, hugging his daughter. He felt Sanne nod and then she pulled away from him.

"That man. He said that it was finished now and he would bring it to a conclusion. And the end would be where it all began" she said as tears welled in her eyes again.

"Where it all began?" Simon asked. She nodded.

Simon stood up and headed towards the exit, where Jonas was still standing.

"Where are you going? Lucy… Sam" Sanne cried.

"My partner here will find them," Simon said, turning to Jonas.

"What are you doing?" Jonas asked.

"I know where he is. I'm going alone"

"Like hell you are. He's dangerous, Simon..." Jonas started, but Simon was out

the door before he had the chance to finish his sentence.

43

Odense, Denmark

It took Simon less than ten minutes to reach the farm. The snow was falling heavy now, and the weather seemed to have stopped everyone from going on the roads. It made it easy for Simon to reach the property, though he was finding it more difficult to control his car.

He parked out the front of the property and looked around. The lights in the main cottage were switched off, but behind the building, he saw a barn.

Nothing looked suspicious about the barn, standing silently in the snow. But Simon thought back to his dreams and felt like a force was pulling him towards the building. He walked through the grass, feeling the cold ice dampen his clothes. As he approached the barn, he noticed it was glowing red. It was on fire.

He picked up the pace now and broke out into a sprint, desperate to reach the building. He didn't even bother to be quiet, he knew he had been heard ages ago. He felt the cold air on his skin as he approached the barn, and as he got closer the ice faded and he was overwhelmed by the heat forcing itself out the property.

At the front of the barn, he saw him. A man, almost seven-foot-tall, holding a shotgun in one hand and watching on as the fire burned.

"This is where it happened," the man said, remaining fixated on the flames.

"You found him here?" Simon asked, already knowing the answer.

"Hanging from the centre of the barn. He was long gone when I cut him down. I burned his body here, so no one would be able to find him. They thought he ran away" the man answered.

"Why the teachers, though? What did they have to do with this?"

"They beat him, tortured him, raped him. They broke him. My father always said that Tobias would earn us money and save us from our business. They robbed us all of a future"

"Elsbet didn't teach at the school during his time there"

"No, but she knew a lot. I had tried to bury it all, but then one day she shows up. Ready to make this all public. I didn't want his name ruined by the media and attention a case like this would get. I didn't want people to know he wasn't just missing but dead. I didn't want his face showing up next to words like rape, torture, and abuse. She gave me the names of the men who did it and with that her purpose was done"

"Erik and Knuv, but that doesn't explain Avilda"

"That woman saw me kill Elsbet, I had no choice. Erik was easy but Knuv, you were one step ahead of me there. I couldn't get to him. With that, I've failed my brother"

"Come with me now, Jørn. It's over" Simon said, grasping the hammer in his pocket.

"And Vibeke – I hope you found her dead" Jørn said, turning to Simon and smiling.

"Vibeke is dead. But she died months ago. The woman you tried to kill was my daughter, Sanne" Simon said. The smile on Jørn's face dropped.

"Tobias told me about Vibeke. About how he told her about the abuse and she did nothing. She watched on, oblivious to it all"

"Vibeke was sixteen. She didn't know any better" Simon said, growing increasingly angry. He felt as though Vibeke was standing with him, defending herself. Jørn held the shotgun under his chin and smiled.

"I'm just glad she's dead," Jørn said, and before Simon had the chance to stop him, Jørn pulled the trigger. The noise filled up the farm but was gone in a split second, the sound of the crackling fire was all that remained.

44

Odense, Denmark

Grief is an element to life that affects everyone in different ways. For most, the grieving process is simple and within weeks' life has begun to move on and tragedies are left as just another fact of life. For most people, it was possible to move on from the worst moments of their lives and carry on for more positive aspects, and it was these people who acted most normally. And then there were those who sank themselves into endless benders with alcohol and loneliness, locking themselves away from the world and absorbing themselves into weeks of self-pity: a complete disregard for their loved ones. Simon had spent much of his time since Vibeke's death in such a state and had only managed to escape from the depression when he was put onto a case that allowed him insight into various forms of other people's grief. There was Avilda, who had mourned her husband for almost fifty years in a way that many would not expect. Rather than marrying again, she became one of the prominent members of the community and did her best to assist others through life. And then June, who had only recently lost her husband to heart disease. Unable to grieve alone, she was back at work almost instantly as she held the very Nordic attitude that life must go on. Simon had envied them their strength, but as he stood watching his daughter being harmed by another grief-stricken individual, he couldn't help but feel as if the past weeks had been almost a blessing.

Upping and leaving for Denmark was certainly an excuse to swallow himself further into depression at first, but it had been through getting back to work and people like Jonas that he had made him lift himself up. But more than anything, it was Vibeke's speaking to him that allowed him to carry on. She had come to him in a dream saying this case was important, and now he knew just how and why. She had known what would bring him happiness and she guided him to it. He didn't have all the answers, but he knew his wife was there for him always.

The sun was beginning to make its appearance as Simon sat in the living room, Sam and Lucy sleeping on either side of him and Sanne staring blankly out the window. He had called into the station to send some cars out to Jørn's farm but had left immediately to be with his daughter. The paramedics had been there when he had returned, but Sanne had refused to go with them to the hospital. They had found Sam and Lucy hiding outside, blue from the cold. Some hot chocolate and blankets later they were back to normal, unaware of what had happened inside. Jonas had told Simon that Sam had gotten angry at his mother for taking to long too find them, and that was when Jonas knew they were fine.

Jonas had also told Simon that Sanne had barely spoken and was clearly in shock. After the paramedics had said she was alright physically, she had insisted all she needed was some rest. Simon could see in his daughter's eyes that she was broken, and he figured they could talk about why Michael wasn't with them later.

Waage had come by to get Simon and Jonas' statements what exactly had happened. He had told them to come into the station the following morning and had then left.

Waage's office was filled with tension. Simon and Jonas sat beside each other and looked on as the Chefpolitiinspektor for Funen paced back and forth behind his desk. He was bright red, and on the edge of his desk sat a pile of papers collected from the investigation. The papers contained everything Simon and Jonas had gathered: police reports, photos of the school, maps of all the attacks, and even an

Odense tourist guide. However, the pile of papers did not contain the one piece of evidence Simon had stolen. He hoped Jonas wouldn't mention it now.

Turning to the two officers, Waage sighed and sat down in front of them. He pulled the papers in front of him and folded his hands on top, pressing the pile down.

"I searched through your documents – there seems to be nothing indicating that Jørn was even a suspect in the investigations. I read your transcripts, I read your police reports, I even read through all the newspaper articles in the hope of finding just one mention of Jørn. But nothing. Jonas, would you care to explain how you decided he was the murderer?" Waage said in a tone that attempted calm, but there was an underlying anger.

"We didn't know it was him, Waage. We thought it was Knuv, the headmaster. We were speaking to him when Simon received an anonymous call." Jonas answered.

"Why was Jørn after you in particular?" Waage said, turning to Simon.

"I don't know. Perhaps he saw my face on the news and didn't understand why a foreigner was investigating. But he threatened my daughter and I traced him to the barn, where he told me about Elsbet and Erik. He also confessed to Avilda. She was a witness to the night Elsbet was killed and Jørn feared she may have seen him"

"But she didn't, though"

"No. He was paranoid and delusional. He was trying to cover his tracks"

"And we are supposed to believe he confessed everything and then killed himself? You didn't kill him in rage?" Waage said, raising an eyebrow.

"I'm just telling you what happened. His brother committed suicide after the abuse at the school. Elsbet had clippings from newspaper articles about the school on her desk. She tipped him off about Erik's involvement and he killed them both."

"Right. Well, fill out your reports and we'll take it from there. That's not to say I believe you" Waage added the second part purposely. He dismissed the men, who left the office rather quickly.

Pulling out a cigarette, Jonas had made his way over to a bench under a tree. Watching a woman trying to coerce her young child to put his winter hat back on as he protested with screams and arm folding, Jonas found himself staring at the innocence of the scene. A mum trying to do what was best for her child through a natural instinct for nurture. Jonas had not seen much of that these past weeks and sighed as he recollected the lies, hurt, and violence that people had inflicted on each other.

As Jonas pulled his phone from his pocket he prepared himself to read the texts that he knew had been coming through from Birgitte these past few hours. As he read the first three it was a taster of how they would all be: emotional, erratic and threatening. She was hurting, he understood that, but he just couldn't bring himself to meet with her. He dreaded having to explain to her that the Odense hero was now under investigation and would probably be fired.

Simon sat down beside him and gave him a single pat on the back.

"I didn't know you smoked" Simon asked.

"I don't," Jonas said, taking a deep breath of smoke.

"Well, it seems we're going to be working together from now on," Simon said, changing the subject.

"Yeah, right. Waage will feed me to the dogs' tomorrow, the old bastard," Jonas scoffed.

"What makes you say that?" Simon said.

"He doesn't believe your story. He thinks you're covering for me"

"You're paranoid," Simon said, but rather than fight it, Jonas sighed and took another breath from his cigarette.

45

Odense, Denmark

Jonas dropped Simon off at the cottage and asked several times if he was sure he didn't want to stay somewhere else, before driving away. Simon went inside and heard the sound of children playing, a welcome sound to the cottage. He saw Sanne sitting on the sofa, watching her children.

Simon noted how young Sanne looked. She looked like the teenager that would keep him up every night. Worrying she was out being destructive. Her face was pale and her eyes were bloodshot. He knew everything had done more damage to her than he was willing to admit.

"This place is so different," Sanne said, looking around at the de struction from the previous night.

"Well, best we sell it then" Simon responded, sitting beside her.

"Where would we live?" Sanne asked, looking to her father. He sensed the sadness in her eyes and put his arm around her.

"What do you mean?" Simon asked.

"Michael left. We're staying here now" was all Sanne was able to say. Simon opened his mouth to ask about Michael, but saw the sadness in his daughters' eyes and decided to leave it for another time.

"We'll keep the house, then. But we'll need new furniture" Simon said. And the two sat there, surrounded by pieces of their mother's memory, broken and thrown around.

Epilogue

Amadej pulled out his semi-automatic from the small drawer which sat at a perfect height to be accessed in a second if needed.

He held it in his hand and extended his arm to point it at the bodyguard standing in front of him. "Bang," he said whilst almost simultaneously laughing at the sheer horror in the giant's eyes and a slight flinch that he tried to immediately rectify.

Amadej enjoyed the power he was holding. "You stupid idiot is that how you think I would waste my time, killing you?! I have plenty of people to do that for me. I have more important things to do. Fuck off out of here. Iść!

The bodyguard counted his steps out of the office and could feel a cold sweat starting to appear on his neck. He felt sick but knew that showing any signs of weakness would cost him his life.

Amadej hated weakness, especially from his staff, and Mateusz knew that he had just marked himself as a target.

As Amadej sat back in his chair he pulled out the pieces of paper from the brown envelope in front of him.

The English bastard owed him a lot of money and had apparently given him the slip. His men had tried to locate him, but after watching his house these last few days, they had sent back reports that Michael and his family had gone.

Amadej pulled out some photos which were sitting in the same envelope as the paperwork. One by one he placed the photos on his desk and put a pin in each one to secure them. The pins went through the foreheads of the faces and Amadej had a feeling of arousal. He didn't like being taken for an idiot, he didn't like some jumped-up English bastard taking his money, and he didn't like his team thinking he was losing his power.

Looking at the photo on the left he took his knife, which always sat on top of his desk, and sliced a straight cut through the middle from left to right. As Simon's head fell from his shoulders, Amadej smiled to himself. The one thing he hated more than people who owed him money was cops. Pigs.

Looking at the pig in the photo, Amadej wondered if pigs squealed when they were slaughtered.

The children who were still in a neat line on his desk also caught his attention. As he tossed Simon's head to the edge of the table he gently pulled the pin from the young girl's forehead. In a floral dress and sandals, she looked every bit the innocent, yet her dad was a fucking thief.

Amadej liked having collateral, as collateral gave him power.

He stood up and headed out of the door. The bodyguard who had acted so cowardly needed some more training, thought Amadej, as he carefully placed the photo of the girl in his pocket for safe keeping.

Coming soon...

THE ENLIGHTENED

The second novel in The Odense Series

When a young girls body is discovered in a burnt-out church, the Odense police initially conclude that it's nothing more than a tragic accident involving a runaway. However, when British detective Simon Weller digs deeper, he finds a link between the girl and a cult up in the most northerly parts of Norway.

As more evidence arises, the arson attack on the church quickly becomes a murder investigation, and sees the detective travelling to Norway to work on the case alongside a young and eager Norwegian counterpart. Everything is not what it seems and they find themselves looking back over the history of Norse Mythology and how the past occult is once again fighting its way into modern day society. Meanwhile, in Odense Simon's colleague Jonas Norgaard discovers an element to the case that puts Simon's life in danger.

As the case unfolds across the corners of Scandinavia, in London Simon's family is falling apart. With her husband, Michael, missing, Simon's daughter Sanne spirals into depression and self-loathing, while her brother Thomas takes care of her children. Frustrated, Thomas starts investigating Michaels disappearance and comes across information that may answer why his mother committed suicide two years ago.

Follow us to keep up-to-date!

www.theodenseseries.com
www.twitter.com/OdenseSeries

THE ENLIGHTENED

SARAH SURGEY · EMMA VESTRHEIM

Lightning Source UK Ltd.
Milton Keynes UK
UKHW010337130922
408763UK00002B/663